MY LADY MISCHIEF

MY LADY MISCHIEF

•

Kathy Carmichael

AVALON BOOKS
NEW YORK

PRINTED IN THE UNITED STATES OF AMERICA
ON ACID-FREE PAPER
BY HADDON CRAFTSMEN, BLOOMSBURG, PENNSYLVANIA

To Robert and Mirna Lynch and my Weathers sibs:
Lisa, Robin, Page and Robert;
and in loving memory of John and Altha Lynch

To my wonderful editor, Erin Cartwright, who gives the perfect
amount of creative freedom mixed with gentle suggestions.
This wouldn't have been a book without her guidance.

To my fellow island dwellers:
Susan Fox, Debby Mayne, and Terry Kanago.
No man is an island and the same can be said of an author.

And always and forever, my love and gratitude to
Andrew, Ian, and John—
who love and encourage me despite the dust bunnies.

Chapter One

Uncle Egbert had become a serious embarrassment. Lady Althea Candler knelt down on the parlor carpet to search beneath the settee. No luck. Uncle Egbert wasn't hiding there.

Thea arose, placed her hands on her hips and scanned the room. Where could he be hiding? He was here in the parlor; she'd chased him into the room moments earlier.

She blew a wisp of hair from her forehead, then brushed at a cobweb on her gown, only slightly aware of how tight it was around her elbows and certain other areas. It had been a very good thing that she'd had the forethought to change into old clothes before going through the attics. Although she hadn't antici-pated a search for Uncle Egbert, it would have put a better gown at risk.

1

Exploring the attics often led to finding hidden treasures. Today she'd discovered one of her deceased mother's old trunks and had retrieved several items that could be put to use. But she hadn't spent as much time going through the trunk as she would have liked. Uncle Egbert was on the loose.

Her gaze fixed upon the tea tray cluttering the room and she shook her head in fond exasperation. Papa had taken tea in the parlor earlier and had ordered the maid to leave it. And, as he was wont to do, once he'd returned to work had forgotten to inform the maid she could clear it away.

Thea abandoned her search for the time and lifted the oval parquetry tray. The delicately flowered Spode china rattled slightly as she adjusted her hold; it was unexpectedly quite heavy. However did the servants manage to carry it so easily?

As she left the room, always on the lookout for a way to save time, she curled her right foot around the door and tugged. The door snapped closed with a reverberating boom, throwing her off balance and causing her to loosen her hold on the tea tray. As it began to slide from her hands, she uttered a phrase she'd often heard her papa use but according to her aunt was not proper for a young woman of class. "Blast it all!"

She winced slightly as the marble-pillared hall echoed her oath, then jumped when a male voice spoke up.

"Allow me."

The tray slid in earnest.

A masculine hand, one she couldn't place in her memory, shot out to provide assistance.

She glanced up to express her gratitude but for once words deserted her.

Clutching the righted tray tightly to her bosom, she stared at the gentleman, from the tips of his glowing Hessian boots to the precise fall of his fashionable cravat. He had deep brown eyes, with laugh crinkles at the lids, a wide mouth, and the breadth of his shoulders was set off perfectly by an impeccably cut coat. His golden blond hair had been arranged around his roughly chiseled face, contrasting with, in a final bit of heavenly perfection, a bold, aristocratic nose.

He was most definitely manly elegance personified. When he bent to retrieve a fallen teacup, Thea stared demurely at the crop of curls covering the back of his head.

"Here you are." He stood, placing the teacup upon her tray.

Had he seen her ogling him? She blushed.

Then he smiled at her and it was all she could do to remember to breathe. Yet, more to the point, what was a veritable pink of the *ton* doing wandering about her household without even a servant accompanying him?

Before she could form the question, a sudden movement caught her attention as she glanced past the gentleman's shoulder. "Uncle Egbert! Fie, I must be after him!"

She dropped the tray upon a table, then sprinted down the corridor. When she realized she was abandoning the gentleman, she turned back. "Won't you care to assist me in my search?"

The gentleman grinned, and she briefly thought that perhaps she should take care to avoid such manly smiles in the future. He dashed to her side. "I thought you'd never ask. Whom are we chasing?"

"Hurry," she said, rounding a corner. "Uncle Egbert. He's been running throughout the house since this morning. Cook says he has to go. I simply must catch him."

She redoubled her efforts, since the pesky fellow had apparently again covered his tracks. "He's getting away!"

Then she spotted him and in a wild grab, she stretched out her arms and dove forward. Unfortunately she connected with empty air and landed headlong upon the floor. The impact knocked the air from her lungs and she watched with dismay as Uncle Egbert darted from sight.

Equally unfortunate, the gentleman hadn't kept up with her sprint and when he rounded the corner, attempted to careen to a halt. This would have normally provided a satisfactory conclusion to a most undignified position, but such was not to be the case. The gentleman tripped over her outstretched feet.

She watched helplessly as he fell directly atop her.

Embarrassed, she shoved at him and he rolled to his feet.

"Are you hurt?" he asked, offering a hand to help her stand. "You won't wish to have your master find you like this."

Although disappointed in her failure to apprehend Uncle Egbert, Thea could barely contain her amusement at the gentleman's misconception. This paragon of manly attributes had mistaken her for a servant!

Thea's sense of humor, often decried by both her papa and Miss Mimms, tended to emerge at the most inappropriate moments. Thea devoutly hoped this wasn't one of those times she'd eventually regret.

The gentleman, however, seemed to expect a response to his statement. She stood, then using as close an approximation as possible to the accents of below stairs, replied, "No, sir."

Amused brown eyes stared into hers. "Surely I deserve a reward? I did my best to aid you in the capture of your uncle."

"Much help you were," she retorted. Then recalling belatedly the role she wished to keep up, she shot him a saucy smile quite like the ones she'd seen exchanged between one of the maids and a handsome footman.

"I'll try to be more helpful next time." The gentleman stepped nearer and Thea fought back an instinctive move to duck as his arms encircled her.

"I suspect my stay here won't be as tedious as I'd feared."

"Hmph." She swatted his arms. As the daughter of an earl, she'd always been protected from gentlemen's advances but, while quite curious about them, wasn't quite ready to totally abandon propriety in the interests of education. Although the most appropriate response for a woman of her class to such behavior was most likely a dainty swoon, Thea was made of sterner material. Besides, her curiosity wasn't quite appeased. "La, sir. What makes you think there will be a next time?"

"I suspect your uncle is a slippery sort of character." The gentleman lowered his head, to steal a kiss Thea suspected. She twisted from his embrace, reeling from the warmth of his touch, which had sent her senses tumbling in a most peculiar manner.

Curious or no, it was best to remove herself, and she retreated toward her Papa's study. Yet, she felt an unexpected regret that she wasn't a servant. She batted her lashes at the gentleman, then asked, "Does my fa— er—master know you're here, sir?"

"No, but I am expected. Come now," he added, matching her step for step, "how about that reward?"

His smile almost, but not quite, scattered her few remaining wits. His gaze mesmerized her and she now understood the fascination of a bird with a cat's stare. Shaking her head to clear the image, she whispered, "I'll announce you. Your name, please?"

"William Cavendar, Marquess of Hartingfield." He watched closely for the housemaid's reaction. Rather than the usual reaction to his name, with the recipient elated by the chance to serve someone of his eminence, the young maid merely cocked a bold brow at him. He rather liked it, but then wondered if some portion of his dress was in disarray, especially after their escapades. His hands shot to check his cravat and coat, but found nothing awkwardly out of order. Even the folds of his cravat remained crisp and unspotted.

What a peculiar servant the girl was. Then he noted the gleam in her eyes and advanced a step toward her. "Most of my acquaintance call me Hart. I would be pleased if you would, too."

A look of shocked awareness crossed her features before she darted into the study, slamming the door in his astonished face.

Heaven's teeth! He'd been stranded in this monstrosity of a house again. Ever since arriving an hour earlier, nothing had happened the way things were supposed to. He'd begun to suspect this was far from a normal household.

Since he'd left his friend Mack to his own devices, the inhabitants of Steyne Hall had gone out of their way to reveal themselves at their most peculiar. First a hysterical housemaid had brought him to this hallway, shrieking something about an uncle running through the kitchens before she'd gone tearing off, stranding him. Next a bareheaded footman had torn past, clutching a powdered wig in his hands. And now this. A bewitching young housemaid, who after attempting to serve tea on his person, had convinced him to chase after her and that demented gentleman named Egbert, only to slam a door in his face.

When had it become his duty to assist young maids in distress? Mack's decision to wait in their rooms for a summons began to seem like the safer choice, if not the wiser.

Hart brushed a nearly invisible dust mote from his sleeve, wondering what the denizens of Steyne Hall would yet arrange to entertain him. An odd feeling, one he hadn't experienced in quite some time, crept over him. At first he had difficulty identifying it. Then it came to him: he was amused.

He wasn't quite sure when it had occurred. Perhaps it had slowly overtaken him when faced with season after season of young hopefuls and pinks of the *ton*. Most assuredly he'd begun to dread another day quite like the day before: a late breakfast, putting in an hour at Jackson's, a stroll through the parks before a night spent partying and gaming. Life seemed lackluster at best. To find amusement, whatever the source, was a rare experience.

At least boredom would no longer be a problem, considering the new experiences he'd encountered since entering this berserk household. Further adventures with the charming housemaid promised delightful entertainment.

How amusing he'd left town in order to avoid the relentless pursuit of matchmaking mamas and their myopic daughters. Little had he suspected that he'd be doing some pursuing of his own, for a decidedly different but far more pleasurable purpose.

Within the study, Thea turned and pressed her back against the door, no longer able to suppress her amusement at the expense of the Marquess. "Your worst nightmare has just been realized, Papa."

"Your aunt has arrived and announced her plans to stay for a fortnight?" asked her father, Bremington Candler, the Earl of Steyne, without looking up from the ledgers on the table in front of him.

"No, Papa." Thea smiled. "You've always warned me about dressing like a servant and now I've been mistaken for one."

"Yes?" This time he looked up and met her gaze.

She nodded. "By none other than Lord Hartingfield. You never told me you'd be having such a rake as a guest."

"Nonsense. He's no more a rake than I was at his age."

"Exactly my point, Papa. Miss Mimms has said—" Thea broke off as he leveled a stare in her direction. "What I mean to say is, I've always suspected you of having a latent propensity toward—"

Her father stood and Thea snapped her lips closed. According to Miss Mimms, this wasn't the sort of thing a young lady discussed with a man, not even her father.

"What did you think of Hartingfield?"

Should she tell him the whole truth? That he'd attempted to steal a kiss? That having him near had stolen her breath? She didn't quite think that would be what her papa would like to hear. There had to be some kernel of truth she could share with him. "He's quite—large."

"Is that all you have to say? His father, the Duke of Devonshrop, wrote me. We were great friends at Oxford, you know."

Thea blinked. Until now, she couldn't recall her father ever mentioning the duke. "I had no idea."

"No." He signed and ran a palm over his balding head as his eyes took on a distracted, saddened appearance. "I don't suppose you did, especially with the quiet way we live here at Steyne. But that will all be changing soon."

If she'd been surprised before, her father's last statement was a total shock. Papa hadn't left Steyne since the death of her mother, years before. "Whatever do you mean?"

"I mean, of course, your upcoming London Season. It's time and past you were presented at court." A gleam of calculation now lit his eyes. "The duke wrote that his health is failing and his heir, Lord Hartingfield, will now be seeking a suitable alliance. It is my belief that you'd make a charming duchess, Thea."

She gasped. "You want me to marry the Duke of Devonshrop, Papa? Isn't he a little—old?"

He gave her a look of pure aggravation. "Not the duke, child, the son. Hartingfield."

"Lord Hartingfield?" He wanted her to marry a veritable libertine? She was scandalized to the pit of her being. "Why, Papa, he's much too free with the ladies."

"Too free with the ladies?" Papa's eyes narrowed. "What *have* you been up to?"

Heat suffused her face. "Me, Papa? Nothing. I haven't been up to anything. I merely refer to rumor."

"Humph," he growled, shooting her a keen glance. "I suspect there's more to this than you're letting on."

She did her best to look demure. It must have proved successful because after a moment, he turned back to his books. Not one to let a chance pass, she took a seat in the chair directly before him. It was the perfect moment to bring up the man she had chosen as an ideal spouse. "Papa, if you wish to discuss prospective marriage partners, I would have thought you'd find Charles Fossbinder imminently suitable."

She watched for a reaction, but was disappointed none appeared. He continued to pore over his accounts.

"If you think on it, I'm sure you'll find the advantages in such a match."

"Nonsense," he scoffed. "Enough of this folderol. The very idea of an earl's daughter, who could look as high as she liked within the *ton*, marrying a farmer's son is preposterous. At any rate, you know Fossbinder will soon be offering for Emma Rawlings and a good alliance it is for both of them."

Thea looked at him in dismay. The conversation was not progressing as she'd hoped. Why couldn't he just accept her choice and leave her to it? Even though her station was far above Charles', she wanted this match. Few gentlemen resided in the area and she longed to remain near Papa, who couldn't look after an insect, let alone himself. Charles would make a perfectly biddable husband. She'd have no trouble from him about what an earl's daughter might or might not do. Papa must come to see the beauty of such an arrangement.

Besides, Emma wasn't in love with Charles. Thea was certain no man had yet claimed her dearest friend's affections. Emma, though, would do as her family bade her, even if that meant marrying the man Thea had set her sights upon. Emma was never one to stand up to anyone.

Something had to be done—finding the means of convincing the earl that his daughter knew her own heart. "Papa, I'm certain if you indicated to Charles that you favored his suit, he'd offer for me."

She bit her lower lip, awaiting his reply.

The earl looked up, considering. As he took in her attire, she realized she looked more like a schoolgirl, or even a servant, than a young woman ready for the responsibilities of matrimony.

He smiled. "I've spoilt you, child. You've had your way too often. You remind me so very much of your lovely mama. I never feel quite so lonely when I see Caroline's eyes beguiling me from your sweet face."

"We both miss her. I'd think that would be all the more reason for you to favor my alliance with Charles, since it would mean I'd remain here at Steyne."

How could she argue with her father when he so obviously loved her and wanted only the best for her? She stood, then walked behind him and curled her arms about his shoulders. "I'm not sure I can bear to leave you."

"Just allow your papa to know best, Thea. It's in the nature of things that a girl should leave her family." He gently swung her to face him. "A London Season will give you the opportunity to meet young men in your own class. In a few short months, you'll forget all about young Charles and be mooning over some pink of the *ton* like Lord Hartingfield."

He brushed back a stray lock of hair from her face. "And though I'll miss you, I'm certain it will be for the best. For both of us."

It was difficult to argue with his logic. Her entire life had centered around Steyne and Steyne Hall. Local assemblies and dances had provided few chances to meet suitable young men. However, only Charles had caught her interest. Although he wasn't her social equal, he was the squire's son and definitely a gentleman. "But Papa—"

The earl silenced her with a kiss on her forehead. "Be off with you to dress for dinner. One of my guests has already mistaken you for a servent. I'd prefer it not happen again."

"Oh, my. I quite forgot."

"What?"

"Lord Hartingfield. He's awaiting you in the hall."

"Heavens. What will he think of us? Show him in."

With a sigh, she walked to the door, giving up on their discussion for the time.

Thea reclined upon an elegant Sheraton rosewood daybed, reflecting on the conversation with her father and her meeting with Lord Hartingfield. The brass fittings of the daybed reflected the late afternoon sun beaming through the sitting room windows.

She sighed. There had been no way she could concentrate on stitches with so much to consider. Miss Mimms, a distant cousin of her father's, stood before a chiffonier, replacing their needlework in one of its many drawers.

Why couldn't she convince her father of the suitability of the match between her and Charles? And why had Lord Hartingfield journeyed to Steyne? What sort of business could Papa have with a man like the marquess?

When Hartingfield had tried to give her a kiss, she'd been tempted to allow it. For a ladies' man to be successful, he had to be devastatingly charming. Hartingfield was that and more. Since Papa seemed set upon sending her to London for a season, she should learn as much as possible about rakes, as Miss Mimms had often told her that the city was full of them.

It was rather fun that he'd mistaken her for a servant. She giggled aloud. "I'm looking forward to dinner this evening, Mimsie."

"Whatever do you find so amusing?" asked the older woman, who had done her best to instill in Thea a modicum of decorum and manners. Miss Mimms' dithery ways engendered in both Thea and her father a mixture of affection and exasperation. However, there were times when she could be quite canny about what motivated Thea. It paid to be cautious when telling the woman about her schemes.

This time, though, Thea decided her intentions were relatively harmless. "Lord Hartingfield is one of our guests. Mimsie, can you imagine? He mistook me for a servant. He'll receive his just reward over dinner this evening when I'm presented to him as the daughter of the house."

"I'm not the least surprised he mistook you for a maid, thanks to the way you carry on, Althea." Miss Mimms fluttered to a comfortable settee adjacent to her. "Hart, here at Steyne? How simply—divine."

Now this was not the reaction she'd expected. "You know him?" Perhaps she could begin her education about men now. "Papa says he will remain with us for a few days."

"We have been introduced, although it has been quite a few years." Miss Mimms rose from the settee and wandered vaguely about the room. "Now, was it at the Billington rout or could it have been at Lady Dillmarsh's ball?"

She bent to plump a cushion. "As I recollect, she was the one who attempted to fire off a silly horse-faced chit, quite sad really, several years ago. A toad eater. That's what the *ton* called her."

"Dear Miss Mimms, it matters not where you were introduced." Miss Mimms had a tendency to wander off on tangents and Thea had to forcibly prevent herself from tagging along with her, although she would have liked to know whether it was the horse-faced chit or her mother who was the toad eater. "Please, tell me what you know about the marquess. Are all London rakes as large as he?"

"Well," Mimms hesitated. "Not to say large. Hart is taller than most, yet I wouldn't think he was the tallest by any means. His manner is most charming and respectable, and he's a thorough-going rapscallion."

She gave a low laugh and Thea could almost picture the woman in her youth. The very idea of her dear cousin possibly being the female version of a rapscallion herself quite alarmed her. It could not be.

"Your Aunt Prunella wrote that his father, the duke, has been ailing for some time. Lady Prunella suspects Hart will soon be looking about for a wife, which may account for his recent popularity with the *ton*. You see, Thea, he has most assiduously avoided matrimony thus far. And you know how every woman adores a challenge."

"Mimms, I greatly fear Papa invited him here because of me," she whispered. The thought made her feel quite unlike herself. If she were the type to become peckish, which she most assuredly was not, she'd be clamoring for a scented handkerchief right now. She took a deep breath. "According to Papa, Hart is indeed looking for a suitable mate. Papa said he's here to discuss business. Yet what sort of business would a London rake have with Papa?"

Mimms looked at her consideringly.

"You don't think Papa would plan an alliance between us without first consulting me, do you?"

"That would not be so odd. Although your parents made a love match, it would not be surprising to find that he planned a match for you." Mimms stared down at her nails. "The marquess is very handsome, comes from a good family, and will soon be the Duke of Devonshrop. Quite a brilliant match for you if your father can bring it off."

"If my father can bring it off? Don't you mean, I?" Thea swung upright and clenched her fists. "And what of Charles? Oh, Mimms. Would Papa completely disregard my feelings?"

"Now that is something best left to your Papa, Althea. Besides, Hart may simply be here to find if you will suit."

Thea felt a strong urge to growl. "If I will suit? What of he? And my father! Selecting a husband for me, as if I haven't sense enough to choose my own?" She hopped from the daybed and began pacing. "I would never have believed it of him."

Mimms looked at her with growing alarm but that didn't deter Thea nor the tantrum she'd worked herself into.

"If I will suit? Why that . . . rake! Kissing a servant without so much as a by-your-leave, while he inspects an earl's daughter as he might a team of grays at Tattersall's!"

Miss Mimms looked at her with growing alarm. "Althea, pray be still. Flinging yourself about this way alarms me. Your papa most likely has other business to transact with Lord Hartingfield. Please recall, our entire conversation is based on conjecture." She rubbed the bridge of her nose. "Even if it is true, you must believe the earl would not compel you to marry against your wishes."

"I had not believed he would arrange a marriage for me without my knowledge, either. Oh, if I am found suitable, perhaps he would force me to marry that loathsome marquess even though he knows I prefer another."

Miss Mimms looked away but her words were meaningful. "Perhaps Lord Hartingfield will find that you do not suit."

Thea stared at Miss Mimms' profile for a long moment, and then seated herself in an armchair near the fire.

When Miss Mimms returned her gaze, Thea wondered if the older woman could guess what was on her mind. She schooled her face to reveal nothing. "Perhaps I will not suit."

"Pray, Althea. You will behave yourself with dignity and restraint."

"Certainly, Mimsie." Her thoughts raced. There must be a way to ensure that Hart would find her most unsuitable. "Certainly."

From the look Miss Mimms gave her, Thea knew the woman had not been reassured.

Chapter Two

In the darkened room, the earl slid the account books away and leaned back in his chair. Rising, he walked over to the large windows looking out on the west lawn. Fiddling with the shutters, he allowed in some light from the late afternoon sun.

Why did Thea want to marry that young whelp, Fossbinder? He was totally unsuitable and even if he were from one of the finest families in all of England, Steyne would object to any match between them.

He walked back to his desk and pulled out a drawer. From beneath several tablets of writing paper, he removed a letter to reread a portion of it.

And so my dear Beamer, I am sending my son to you under the auspices of discussing land. If he and your girl, Lady Althea, do not hit if off,

18

*I suppose I shall be forced into arranging a mar-
riage for him. However, I believe any daughter
of Caroline's must be sublime, even if you are
her father!*

*So throw them together, old sport. Let's see if
Caroline's daughter can do what no other belle
of the ton has yet been able to do—entice my son
into marriage. Throw them together and let's see
if the sparks fly!*

Well, the earl thought, sparks were certainly flying
but he wasn't certain they were the right sort. What
was it she'd called Hart? A rake? And hadn't she
claimed he was too free with the ladies?

When he and Squigy, the duke, had been young
men together, he felt certain all the matrons in London
had warned their daughters against them. Steyne
laughed in recollection of the larks and sprees they'd
been up to together. But it had all ended upon their
marriages.

His marriage to Caroline and Steyne's to Lady
Anne. The two men-about-town had been speedily reformed by their spouses. Where once they'd been
wild, now they were both quite sedate and conceivably
boring. For himself, he'd discovered the joy of country
living and the simple pleasures of breeding prize winning pigs. Squigy had become dry to the point of being
brittle.

No. He couldn't believe Hart's current behavior was
indicative of how he'd act once suitably leg-shackled.

Close proximity with Fossbinder had never created
the glow Thea developed after spending those few mo-

ments with Hart. Not to mention her betraying blush. Being a rake could be an advantage when it came time to court a young lady.

Caroline would have been proud to think her daughter might be Duchess of Devonshrop. Squigy had courted her but Caroline had married Steyne instead, choosing love over a dukedom. Now, her daughter had a chance at the title she had declined. He hoped Thea could have both.

Returning the letter to the drawer, Steyne thought back over his years with Caroline, the happiness and the sadness. With a sharp stab of grief, he recalled the two stillborn sons who lay entombed beside his dearest Caroline in the family vault.

How elated they'd been when Thea was born healthy, screaming for attention. By then, they'd been a bit long in the tooth for starting a family. They had been so proud and pleased to behold their delightful baby daughter.

He'd never forget the loving look of wonder on Caroline's face as she nursed Thea for the first time. It had been the mode to retain a wet nurse but Caroline would hear nothing of it. He could still hear her sweet voice saying, "This baby is healthy and I am determined to keep her that way."

Now, their beautiful daughter was a young woman, ready to fall in love. He hoped Caroline approved of the way he'd raised her. Yes, the child was spoiled but surely she knew she was loved and cared for. That could not be harmful.

"You would be so pleased, Caroline," he whispered fervently. "I just hope you are watching. You'll have to help me not to botch matters."

He sincerely hoped Thea and Hart would come together on their own, but he wasn't above doing a little
something to encourage them in that direction. With
any luck, that scoundrel Fossbinder would soon be out
of the picture.

"I promise you, Hobbs, when we left London I had
no idea I'd need your services." Hart stood before the
dresser in his room at Steyne Hall while his offended
valet fluttered about, preparing for the evening ahead.
From the corner of his eye, Hart watched to see if his
flattery had any effect. "Lord Steyne informed me we
would be dressing for dinner, and I can never accom-
plish a creditable appearance without your assistance.
I'm relieved you insisted upon accompanying Mack
and me. Though why you don't insist upon attending
Mack?"

"He's an American, my lord," commented the valet
in a dry voice. "Quite able to take care of himself."

Hart wondered why the sentiment had never occurred to him. An American could dress himself, yet
a marquess could not. An interesting opinion but not
one that he shared. "Well, I'm pleased you're here."

Hobbs snorted into a handkerchief. "No use trying
to turn me up sweet, your highness. Sneaking off that
way, without even a clean shirt in your kit."

It was clear the Scot would not easily be appeased.
Hart suppressed a sigh. "At least we've reached the
point where you are again speaking to me. What can
I do to regain your good graces?"

The valet responded by turning his back. Hart had
spoken too soon.

Hart tossed down his third neckcloth, then gingerly inspected the crisply starched one his valet now condescended to offer. Though Hobbs' relationship with him was not the typical one shared between master and servant, he believed matters had gone far enough. It was time to put an end to the valet's sulks.

"At least the earl appears interested in Mack's seed drill improvements." He cringed as his servant let out a reverberating sneeze, then offered him a fresh handkerchief.

Hobbs wiped his nose in offended silence. Since Hart's childhood, the valet had been fanatically loyal and was privy to his innermost plans. How could Hart be angry over such devotion to duty and to himself?

"When my father requested I visit Steyne about the land he hopes to acquire, he mentioned the earl might be interested in Mack's new process." He felt certain this would lure the valet back to speech, especially since Hobbs considered Mack an influence for the better, even if he was an American.

Hobbs merely grunted.

Since that hadn't worked, he'd have to attempt another method. In an intentionally bored voice, he said, "Yet, now I have to play the pretty when all I'd really like is more time trading barbs with that feisty parlormaid. Have you discovered anything more about her?" Surely this would draw him out.

Hobbs swiped at his nose and replied without recollecting that he was not on speaking terms with his master. "Must be new in the household, my lord. No one seems to know the first thing about the chit. May be something rummish about her since the servants all mum up when I mention her." The valet suddenly clamped his mouth shut and resumed his affronted attitude.

He lofted a blue silk dress coat, then eased it on his master as quickly as its snug fit would allow. This tedious chore completed, Hobbs pulled the long lace wrist-ruffles into place from beneath the coat sleeves.

While giving himself up to the valet's ministrations, Hart's mind began to wander back onto the subject of the parlormaid. She was a prime article, quite unlike the maids who served in his own household. The moment she'd spent in his arms had been a pleasurable experience and he looked forward to repeating it. Trifling with parlormaids was not in his usual style, but he found himself unable to get the young woman out of his mind.

He looked sidelong at Hobbs, who had yet to come out of his snit. What would it take to make the man come around? Hart was generally on friendly terms with his servants and truly regretted the impulse that had led him to try elude Hobbs when he left town. The man had been suffering a tremendous head cold. What else could Hart have done?

"It would be comforting to experience a little gratitude," Hobbs growled. At last, Hart saw a slight grimace on the older man's face. This had hit home! "Hobbs, I am indeed sorry for trying to leave you. You were ill, man. Just look at you now, snuffling and sneezing fit to blow the walls down. You do understand?"

"Aye, my lord."

Hart breathed a sigh of relief, but then Hobbs looked him directly in the eyes.

"I tell ye now, sir, there is something odd about yon parlormaid. Watch out for yerself."

Hart laughed, delighted that the old Hobbs had returned, heathen Scots' accent and all. Thinking of the chit again, he came to a decision. After dinner, he would seek her out.

Putting the finishing touches to his neckcloth, he completed a perfect Waterfall. "You worry too much, Hobbs. And I thank you for it." He clasped his man's shoulder in a tiny squeeze, then scooped up his gloves and left the room.

Once the door closed, Hobbs whispered, "And if I don't worry about ye, who else will?"

It had been difficult to come up with a plan, thought Thea, but after a period of reflection, a solution had occurred to her. If Lord Hartingfield's purpose at Steyne was to ascertain her suitability as a wife, then she knew what she must do to put an end to such a notion.

Standing before her wardrobe, she took particular care in selecting appropriate dinner garb with her abigail, Meg's, assistance. Miss Mimms had previously stressed the need for creating the right impression, and for once Thea found herself in complete agreement. She grinned, assured Miss Mimms might have succumbed to the vapors had she known just what sort of impression Thea wished to create.

She dismissed several evening gowns as too prim, then finally settled upon a new gown that had been acquired for her dreaded upcoming London Season.

Though she'd done everything in her power to dissuade both Papa and Miss Mimms from such a concept, they'd insisted upon her acquiring at least a partial wardrobe.

With judicious removal of the lace at the bodice, Thea was pleased with the now plunging neckline. Her time had been well spent. "I regret the fact I haven't anything truly vulgar to wear, like Mrs. Twining over at the Rose and Crown."

"She's no Missus, if you take my meaning," replied Meg as she held up a new bit of lace to Thea's bodice. "Any course, his Lordship would be very upset to hear you speak of her, Miss."

She thrust the fabric back into Meg's hands. "I have no intention of using this."

"Oh, Miss. Whatever will Miss Mimms say?" moaned Meg. "You never mean to go downstairs dressed like that. You simply must add some lace to that gown."

"Nonsense," Thea replied with a puckish grin. Meg's distress was obvious. She was a young village girl whom Thea had taken in to train as her dresser. She was genuinely fond of the girl and deemed their arrangement successful in spite of Meg's outspokenness.

Turning to check her image in the glass, Thea noted that the gown came a bit above her ankles and felt quite daring. The white gown of India muslin was adorned with dark green flowers on the lower panel and the puffed sleeves. A matching green ribbon encircled her waistline, just below her generously exposed neckline. She looked positively bold, just the image she wished to achieve.

"It's relieved I am, Miss, that you didn't dampen your petticoats. I'm thinking you'd be happier if you wore some stays and an extra petticoat. You look like a lady who is no better than she should be—begging your pardon, Miss."

"That was my intention, Meg. Look at the way this gown clings." She practiced a gentle sway, then nodded her head at her image, assured this would change Lord Hartingfield's mind about her suitability.

"Do I indeed look vulgar, Meg?" She grinned wickedly. "Enough to curtail any thoughts of marriage the marquess may be entertaining?"

Meg collapsed upon a chair with another moan while Thea donned a pair of matching green elbow-length gloves. Flashing the abigail a supplicating smile, she turned to make a final adjustment to her hair, styled *a la Caracella*, a few long ringlets draped upon one shoulder. She'd come across a number of carefully preserved peacock feathers in her mama's trunks and had attached them to the wide ribbon that held her hairstyle in place.

Selecting the delightfully low Mrs. Twining as a model had been a perverse inspiration, for her appearance was all that could be desired. "Do not despair, Meg. I know what I am about. When Lord Hartingfield learns my identity, the last thing he will wish for is marriage. Miss Mimms has assured me that gentlemen do not marry wantons."

"What they do with 'em is what worries me, Miss Althea. That and losing my position."

Although tempted to learn more about what gentlemen did with wantons, Thea realized she didn't have time for any discussion about the matter. She had a date with destiny. "Nonsense, Meg. Cheer up. I'm certain I've considered every possible thing that can go wrong and my plan is unassailable."

Thea peered into the drawing room and found, much to her relief, that it was empty. She wanted time to set an appropriate scene before meeting Lord Hartingfield. Feathers bouncing, she darted over to the fire in the massive grate, thankful for the warmth it provided in the chilly room. Her revealing attire did not give the same protection from drafts as her normal clothing. How fortunate her petticoats had not been dampened, for by now she would have been forced to return to her rooms for a wrap.

She heard footsteps approaching and quickly took up a pose she hoped would be perceived as risque. It wouldn't do to have Lord Hartingfield find her shivering like a green girl, not if she wished him to believe her to be anything other than what she truly was—a miss barely out of the schoolroom.

A man's silhouette was visible and she quickly looked away, feigning indifference. Her heart pounded in her chest and she hoped the sound was not audible to anyone other than herself.

"Thea, how are you this evening, m'dear?"

She had difficultly suppressing a nervous start, for the voice was her father's. Her plan had encompassed every eventuality but she'd forgotten one very important consideration. What would her father think of her immodest apparel? She cleared her throat. "I'm very well, Papa."

He stepped into the light and his brow furrowed as he eyed her ensemble. She watched as the furrow turned into a look of disbelief and then a scowl. Biting her lip, she stood a bit straighter, hoping to somehow pass his inspection. Drat it all, why hadn't she considered what his reaction would be when he caught sight of her? Perhaps she could carry it off if she conducted herself as if nothing was untoward?

"Althea Emogene Candler," the earl growled.

With his use of her full name, Thea knew she would be lucky to get out of this predicament with her skin intact.

"You will return to your room at once. I will have dinner sent up to you." He sputtered to a halt, apparently unable to find the proper words to express his disapproval. Thea sagged.

Chapter Three

On the landing above the open doorway, Harting-field carefully flicked a speck of lint from his waistcoat before slowly descending the center stairwell. The sound of voices drew him to the drawing room.

The earl's voice rang out, "I do not know what ploy you had in mind, Thea, but it will not work. Be off with you."

Hartingfield stepped in the doorway, taking stock of the situation, then spied Lord Steyne standing near the fire. As a young woman headed in his direction, he stepped back to allow her exit. When she passed, he recognized her—his parlormaid.

Earlier she'd been dressed like a typical, although slovenly, servant. Now, however, her appearance had undergone a thorough transformation. She was attired in a manner that might only be politely described as garish. He was particularly struck by the seven glitter-encrusted peacock plumes dancing drunkenly about her head.

Realizing she was about to escape, Hart scrambled through the hall and up the stairwell. Just as she reached the landing, he clasped her arm and she whirled about, startled. One of the peacock plumes was dislodged by the sudden motion and it leaned forward over her head, like a fan held over a pharaoh.

Ignoring the feather, she glared at him and asked haughtily, "Did you require something, your lordship?"

His jaw tightened. Her arrogant attitude began to grate. Without pausing to consider, he blurted out, "Are you under Lord Steyne's protection?"

She peered at him uncertainly then drew herself up. "At this moment, I fear I need someone to protect me from Lord Steyne!"

His gaze fell to her exposed décolletage. She cleared her throat and he realized he'd been staring far too long. Gadzooks, he was behaving like a cawker. Hadn't he seen many women far more scantily clad? Why should *she* hold such fascination?

He led her abruptly into a small alcove off the landing. "Are you happy in your situation here?"

She looked at him in surprise, opening and shutting her mouth without uttering a sound.

He removed his hand from her arm and brought it to encircle her slim waist. She was the most distracting creature he'd come across in years. Hopefully he'd soon make a propitious arrangement with her. Although he felt a little guilt over the idea of stealing his host's lady bird out from under his nose, Hart simply couldn't resist the appeal of her charm. And she did appear to be unhappy.

He gently massaged her ribcage and he heard her breath quicken. Reassured by her response, he asked, "Would you consider a change? A change in situation?"

Recalling the earl's words, Hart tilted his head toward the drawing room. "You would not need to use ploys with me. I would take very good care of you."

His Botticelli beauty's face infused with color and she jerked from his embrace. "You and my father would like that, wouldn't you?"

"Your father?" Just what did her father have to do with it, unless he arranged his daughter's liaisons? The poor thing must have had a rough time of it. He resolved to make it up to her, to provide her with every luxury that his income could provide.

He was brought back to the moment when she jabbed him in the chest with her forefinger.

"And you, you oaf," she said through clenched teeth. "You neither know nor care about me in the least. Why should you? You men are all alike." She jabbed him again.

"We women are merely chattel, to be traded or bartered as men deem fit. Well, I won't have it, and you won't have me! I cannot bel—"

Hartingfield cut her off by clamping his lips upon hers, effectively silencing the vixen's tirade and halting the bruising of his chest in one swift move. At first, she held herself rigidly, but that was not difficult for a man of his experience to overcome. He softened his kiss and she yielded to his entreaty. After a moment of great satisfaction, he relaxed his hold upon her. "I am offering you carte blanche."

Again she yanked away from him, her eyes lit like an inferno as two more plumes flew out of place, lodging above each shoulder. Another plume dropped to the ground. "When pigs fly, my lord!"

At the same instant, each bent to retrieve the feather, resulting in a great knocking of heads.

Thea stood back up and waited, hand outstretched for Hart to deliver the plume. After he handed her the feather, she left the alcove and marched down the passageway, the two plumes prancing behind her with military precision at each step she took.

"Please stay," coaxed Hart with a laugh in his voice. She did not stop. He didn't follow her, his amused gaze fastening to the trail of glitter drifting in her wake.

It had been rather surprising when she hadn't jumped at his offer. Possibly she didn't fully understand the ramifications? After all, he'd neglected to sweeten the pot by offering to take her to London to the townhouse that would be her own.

She didn't behave like any servant or woman he'd ever known, and that was part of her attraction. At least he knew her name, Thea, and that she was not indifferent to him. Her kiss had been pure heaven. Surely it was just a matter of time before he could claim her as his own. He'd have to request Hobbs to look into introducing him to Thea's father.

The back of his neck prickled. Turning, he looked to his left. From the corner of his eye, he thought he'd seen a curly white wig perched atop the features of a pig. Surely not.

He shook his head to clear his vision but kept his eyes on the doorway. Just then Mack, Paul McCormack, came around the corner. Hart blinked a few times, then asked, "Did you just see a—? No. Never mind."

Resolved to relegate Thea and the phantom pig to the back of his mind, he smiled warmly at his American friend. "Good news, Mack. Lord Steyne has expressed interest in your drill improvements. His purchase of the process should serve you well."

Mack clapped him on the back. "It is very good of you to go to so much trouble for me."

"You've never failed me. What reason would there be for me to fail you now?" Hart felt uncomfortable with Mack's expressions of gratitude, for what were friends for, if not to aid one another? "Shall we seek out our host?"

Thea was infuriated with herself and most particularly infuriated by Lord Hartingfield. Primarily, she couldn't believe she'd acted in such a brazen manner. At one touch of his lips, she'd nearly swooned into his arms. The cad hadn't even been offering marriage as she'd thought, he'd offered to make her his mistress! At least she was safe from him and from herself here in her room.

After returning to her suite, she'd quickly discarded the costume that had influenced her to act in such an unladylike manner. A footman had delivered her dinner but she'd been unable to eat more than a bite or two.

Now she paced, back and forth, back and forth. Surely Lord Hartingfield knew he offered her, the daughter of an earl, an insult? He'd obviously overheard their conversation. She threw up her hands. Men.

That's why Charles was so perfect for her. He never behaved in an unexpected manner, he hadn't even attempted to kiss her. For the first time, she wondered why. Heavens, he did find her attractive, didn't he?

She hoped he didn't sense what she hadn't realized until tonight, that she was a libertine in fine clothing. Sinking onto her bed, she chewed her thumbnail, hoping Miss Mimms wouldn't notice, for she'd spent the entire previous summer helping her overcome this dreadful habit.

It was possible Lord Hartingfield had offered her the insult deliberately, in an attempt to make her grateful for a legitimate offer of wedlock. He didn't know his woman if he thought such ploys would work with her.

Thea jumped up and resumed her pacing, more determined that ever to put the arrogant marquess in his place.

When the next day dawned bright and clear, Thea resolved to put yesterday's calamities behind her by proceeding with her normal schedule. Accordingly, she'd gone to the kitchens and stood in conversation with the cook at Steyne Hall, Mrs. Smith. Things were not progressing as she'd hoped.

"Oh, please, Mrs. Smith. Papa must never find out about Uncle Egbert." She stooped to place a squirming piglet in her basket on the table. The aroma of freshly baked bread gave added appeal and a sense of security to the well-organized kitchen.

"You just make sure to keep that animal out of my kitchen, Missy. I am that busy, with guests in the house, I'd as lief not interrupt my schedule for a visit with his lordship." Mrs. Smith had ruled the pantry since long before Thea's birth. She'd administered cookies and hugs to her, and instigated the only discipline she'd ever known.

Thea threw her arms around the matronly woman. "Thank you, Mrs. Smith." The piglet and basket almost went flying. Releasing the cook, she steadied her basket. "I knew I could depend upon you. Should Papa discover I adopted one of his prize piglets, I'm certain he'd have apoplexy." She gazed down at the warm pink pig and tickled his chin. "Isn't he the most darling pet?"

"That darling pet is a nuisance and a menace. He'll soon be weighing more than you, Miss, and don't you forget it."

Carrying her basket and piglet, Thea walked toward the door as Mrs. Smith called out, "You'd best return that pig to his mama, Lady Althea, where he belongs."

Mrs. Smith simply didn't understand, thought Thea, as she wandered through the kitchen gardens to make her way to the barns. She cooed to her piglet, "Papa said I might have a kitten or a puppy as a pet, dear one. But they are too ordinary, aren't they?"

Uncle Egbert grunted a piggish answer.

"You, my precious, need someone to look after you. Being the runt of the litter is never easy. It's no wonder the others mistreat you since you are so much more clever than they. I'll do my best to help you, but you'll have to behave. No more roaming through the house or persisting with your practical jokes, or we'll both find ourselves in the suds."

She eyed the piglet, looking to see if he were indeed the reincarnation of Uncle Egbert, as Miss Mimms asserted. They did share a number of common traits, but surely it wasn't possible. Her piglet was simply more clever and amusing than the run-of-the-mill variety.

Reaching the barns, she set down the basket and slipped a ribbon from her hair. "There, dear, this will set you apart from your greedy brothers." She carefully tied a bow about his neck. The grey circle surrounding his left eye, as well as his small size, also set him apart, but she hated to mention it for fear he might be sensitive about the subject. She planted a kiss on his rosebud snout then nudged him into place beside his mother.

From there, basket swinging from her arm, Thea ambled into the flower garden. In a few short months, the rosebushes would be covered in glorious blooms. She had hoped to be wed to Charles by that time. Papa was being awfully difficult to convince. She suspected that a portion of his disapproval was based upon his animosity toward Charles' father, Squire Fossbinder. The long-term resentment had been founded upon a competition between the two men over who produced the finest pigs in the county.

Recently, a misunderstanding had arisen about the paternity of one of the squire's litters. The earl suspected that, without his permission, the squire had used one of his pigs as stud. Tensions had escalated as a result, along with threats of legal charges of pig-napping and slander.

However, the Fossbinders were the Candlers' closest neighbors and it was necessary that a truce prevail, unhappy though it might be. Each gentleman delighted in trading barbs and digs at the other's expense while maintaining a falsely friendly relationship. Thus, it was doubly difficult for Thea to convince her Papa to accept Charles as her suitor. To Papa, the squire was untrustworthy and therefore it followed that the squire's son was as well.

None of her previous plans to persuade her father had succeeded. As she tried to fix on a new strategy, she gathered the daffodils that bloomed profusely on this sun-filled morning.

After placing an especially beautiful blossom in her basket, Thea heard the scrunch of footsteps upon gravel and looked up to see an oddly dressed man approaching. Instead of the usual top hat, or even a bicorne, his hat was flat-crowned and broad-brimmed. And, although there was nothing particularly wrong about his clothing, there was a decided difference which she could not define.

Thea realized this must be their American guest, Mr. Paul McCormack.

He was an attractive man, of average height but with a very erect stance which made him appear quite tall. He removed his hat and his brown hair ruffled in the light breeze as his mild blue eyes smiled in greeting.

"How do you do?" Thea asked. "You must be our American."

With an amused bow, he answered, "Yes, indeed. I am Paul McCormack. At dinner last night, Lord Steyne mentioned a young daughter, Lady Althea. Might you be her governess?"

Thea smiled. "I am the earl's daughter, Althea Candler."

"You are his little dumpling?" he spluttered, then threw back his head in a laugh. "The way he described you, I thought you'd still be in the nursery."

With a laugh she replied, "Papa still speaks of me as if I were a child." Thea tilted her head. "Is this your first visit to England?"

"No, I spent some time here at Oxford and also as a youth, with my grandfather. But that was many years ago."

She decided she liked his soft, accented speech and gentle grin. "Do you plan to remain in England?"

"No, my grandfather is deceased and my immediate family is in America. Although I'm unsure how long I will remain, it is my intention to return home at some point."

"Thea!" A feminine cry rang out. Recognizing the voice of her dearest friend and confidant, Emma Rawlings, Thea peeked around a shrub and waved to her friend to join them.

Emma's golden hair, which had been pulled back with a ribbon, was windswept and sweetness glowed from her cheery face. She was the daughter of the vicar who held the living at Steyne. Since the Rawlings' income was limited, as a young girl Thea had been pleased to share her governesses and tutors with Emma, resulting in an even closer friendship.

Recalling her manners, Thea introduced her friend to the young man. Mr. McCormack bowed gallantly. "It is a pleasure to meet another lovely English blossom, Miss Rawlings."

Emma's dimples peeped out as she returned a curtsey.

The threesome continued strolling and chatting in the gardens. Yet all the while, Thea observed with some bewilderment, Emma sent out strange hand signals to her behind the gentleman's back. The young woman continued pantomiming until a footman approached, beckoning to Mr. McCormack.

He took a note from the silver salver which the footman offered, then scanned it. "I look forward to furthering our acquaintance, Lady Althea, Miss Rawlings." He winked at Miss Emma Rawlings as he said, "Unfortunately I have been summoned but I hope to see you both again soon." After executing a polite bow, he followed the footman from the gardens.

As soon as he was gone, Emma unceremoniously plunked Thea down upon a garden seat.

"We must talk, Thea," Emma said in an undertone, glancing about to see that they could not be overheard.

"Pooh, Emma. Whyever are you behaving so peculiarly?"

Emma straightened her shoulders. "This is a terribly serious subject and one that is most difficult to broach.

Before I begin, you must promise you will divulge this to no one."

"I am surprised at you, Emma. Did I tell about the time you fed Mrs. Tompkins' fresh cherry pie to the sparrows? You know I am not one to talk." Thea studiously smoothed her skirts and trained wide eyes upon her agitated friend. "Now spill the soup before I perish of curiosity."

Chapter Four

Thea studiously smoothed her skirts and fixed her eyes upon her agitated friend.

"I have previously informed you about the attentions Mr. Charles Fossbinder has been paying me." Emma peeped at Thea through downturned lashes.

Thea froze, certain that the moment she'd been dreading had arrived. Emma and Charles must be betrothed! "Go on," she said through stiff lips.

"Last evening, Charles was closeted with my father for over an hour. This morning my mother has hinted that he received Father's blessing to proceed with his suit." Emma placed the back of one hand to her brow as silent tears dripped down her face. "She then reminded me of my duty to the family and to my brothers. Father must soon settle an allowance on them and

41

he would be rid of the expense of my upkeep." The dam broke and Emma began to sob in earnest.

"Oh, no." Thea's distress colored her words as she pulled Emma's head down upon her shoulder. "How could they be so cruel to one as sweet as you?"

Sobbing into Thea's shoulder, Emma mumbled, "You are aware of my fondness for Charles but I cannot bear the thought of achieving my happiness at your cost. And I have not forgotten our promise to marry brothers so that we may be sisters."

Emma dug in her reticule for a handkerchief. Thea, knowing her companion would never find one, removed her own from her sleeve and handed it to the distraught young woman.

"That was a mere childhood fancy, Emma. But I will always remain your sister, in thought if not in matrimony."

After her emotional storm abated somewhat, Emma dried her eyes. "Did you have an opportunity to speak with your father about Charles?"

Thea nodded. "The situation seems hopeless. Papa has insisted upon my having a season in London. If after that, Charles is still unwed, I might have a chance of bending Papa's mind." Thea turned away from Emma, her voice breaking.

"I suspect Papa may be arranging a marriage of convenience for me." She stoically lifted her chin. "In that event, I know I shall expire of anguish."

Emma grasped Thea's hands in her own. "Surely your father does not wish to make you miserable." Choking back another sob, Emma stood and raised plump hands to her bosom. "How could the fates have been so cruel—to give us families whose worldly ambitions are more important to them than their daughters' own happiness? Whatever shall we do?"

"You, Emma, must accept Charles' offer." Thea spoke with conviction in her voice, drawing strength from the depth of her feelings for Emma and the knowledge of her own virtuous sacrifice. "At least one of us shall achieve true happiness."

"Oh, Thea, you are so good, so fine. However did I earn such a friendship as yours?" Placing one hand over her heart, Emma pledged, "You shall be named as godmother to my first child."

Thea calmly accepted the pledge as her due. "You are truly kind, my sister." Feeling guilty because she could not rid herself of the slight hope that something might develop to reverse the situation, she reminded herself that she cared too much for Emma to be jealous of her good fortune. "For you and Charles to be blissfully happy shall be my greatest reward."

After knocking heartily upon the door, Mack entered Hart's bedchamber to observe his friend's head looming above a screen separating the dressing area from the sleeping portion of the room. Dominating the latter area was a massively majestic velvet-tasselled four-poster bed. Mack cautiously took a seat upon it while noting its ornate embellishments.

"Have you just arisen, Hart?"

"Up with the worms again?" Hart replied waspishly. "I had forgotten your vulgar foreign ways."

"Please accept my apologies for disturbing you, your lordship," Mack said with a grin that belied his sarcastic tone. "Lord Steyne awaits us. Put a spur on, will you?"

Hart and his valet continued the arduous process of properly outfitting his person in a manner befitting a country gentleman. Mack grimaced at the sight of Hobbs' face. The valet's left eye was nearly swollen shut.

"Did you run into Hart's fist, Hobbs?"

Hart chuckled as Hobbs replied grimly, "No, Mr. Mack. I was making inquiries, at his lordship's command, pertaining to the toothsome maid in whom he has taken an interest."

"And you call yourself a gentleman, Hart. I thought you would be too high in the instep for a mere servant." Mack turned to Hobbs. "Her inamorata objected?"

"No," was Hobbs' response. His carefully cultivated diction began to deteriorate as his agitation grew. "I'm not really sure of the right of it, Mr. Mack. There we were, me an' the upper footman, getting along all right and tight when I coyly popped in a question about the earl's fair Paphian, known as Thea. Next I know, the fellow's muggers come up and he blackens me ogler. Never seen the like of it afore. No explanation nor nothing."

Mack bit his tongue to keep from laughing. Lady Althea a fair Paphian, indeed! What deviltry had Hart been up to anyway? And with the earl's daughter of all people. He reclined on the bed and crossed his legs, finding himself mesmerized by the detail on the tester overhead.

"Care to let us in on the joke, Mack?"

His attempts to keep a straight face must have been less than successful. "No. I can't perceive what you've been about, Hart, unless you're a bit foggy in your upperworks." He smiled a reassuring grin. "However, you will come around to it in time, I'm sure." Glancing up once more, he asked with awe, "How can you get any rest in this monstrosity?"

Hart smiled. "It hasn't been easy. Now be off with you and let me complete my toilette in peace."

Mack arose from the bed with èlan. "Certainly, your lordship," he said with a deep bow suitable for the Prince Regent. "I will await you in the estate room." He closed the door as he left.

Hart could hear Mack's guffaw through the thick oaken door separating them. Turning to his valet, he asked, "What do you think that was about?"

"I can't be sure, sir, but I still suspicion something about that parlormaid of yours."

Thea's foot rested on the topmost step, where it had remained immobile for some moments while she mentally prepared to join their guests for supper.

Generally, she wasn't this indecisive. Her previous scheme to force Hart to reject her as a possible spouse hadn't come off as she'd hoped. Now, she had to face him again and couldn't keep memories of his kiss from intruding on her thoughts. Did all young women who were kissed feel this way or was there something unusual about her? Miss Mimms had said that young ladies didn't allow men to accost their person. Perhaps this was what she meant. Hart's kiss had certainly felt like an assault, at least to her senses. She'd never anticipated such a reaction from merely pressing a gentleman's lips to her own.

She bit her lip. She'd learned something from this scheme of hers. If one touch of a rake's lips made her want to throw away years of training, was she no better than Mrs. Twining? Blood rushed to her face.

Nonsense, she scolded herself. The marquess hadn't known who she was when they'd last met. Could she use his mistake to her advantage? Hart most definitely wouldn't want an abandoned woman as his new Marchioness. If only she could get through this evening without causing him to revise his opinion of her.

Yet, she had to keep her father in mind. This evening, she'd dressed in a manner in which he would most assuredly approve. The butterflies dancing in her stomach began to annoy her.

"Good evening, Lady Althea."

Turning, she recognized Mr. McCormack. He extended an arm and she placed her hand on it for him to escort her down the stairway. "Thank you."

A playful smile lit his face as he bent down to say, "I'm very much looking forward to the coming introductions."

She peeped at him. "You are?"

He laughed. "I can't wait to see Hart's face."

Hart. That seemed appropriate. But this must mean Mr. McCormack knew that Hartingfield hadn't yet penetrated her identity. "What do you mean?"

"Don't play your jests on me, Lady *Thea*, for I'm sure you had much to do with it."

She paused to frame her reply. "Not to say I deliberately misled him."

This time Mr. McCormack guffawed and slapped his thigh. "You're up to all the larks, aren't you? I'm willing to bet you didn't deliberately educate him, either."

Thea grinned at him. "It has been rather fun. Why didn't you tell him?"

"What, and miss the sport?" He shook his head. "Never."

They entered the drawing room. Thea's gaze went directly to Lord Hartingfield where he stood beside the hearth. She barely noticed the look of approval her father directed at her. Miss Mimms sat beside him and nodded happily.

No, she had eyes only for Hart. If she'd thought him handsome before, she was even more impressed seeing him in evening dress. Dismissing an urge to turn and hide, she straightened her chin.

Mr. McCormack placed his hand over hers and dragged her toward the marquess. "May I have the pleasure of introducing our host's daughter, Hart?"

"Lady Althea, I'm happy to present Lord Hartingfield." Mr. McCormack dropped her arm and stepped back.

Thea curtsied as Hart bowed.

"How do you do," said Hart in a perfunctory tone. Rising from his low bow, he glanced up and directly into her eyes. She grinned at his look of astonishment. "Good heavens! The parlormaid."

"I've been eagerly awaiting this moment, my lord." Thea batted her lashes at him and was happy to note his discomfort. After the offer he made, this come-uppance was justly deserved. "Had you no suspicion?

I was certain Mr. McCormack would have enlightened you."

"He obviously felt it too good a joke to share, Lady Althea." As if unwilling to allow her such an easy victory, he asked, "Do you frequent masquerades?"

Thea felt her color rise. Then she gleamed wickedly at him. "Do you always make advances to parlor-maids, my lord?"

"Do you never discourage such advances?"

"Touché, Lord Hartingfield," said Thea with a laugh. He'd hit rather close to home on that one.

"*I do begin to perceive that I am made an ass.*" He shot her an ironic smile.

"Indeed, my lord." She recognized the quotation from Shakespeare. At least the cur was well-read. In spite of her desire to put him on the spot, her lips twitched in appreciation. "*Egregiously an ass,*" she quipped back.

"Please accept my apologies, Lady Althea." Despite his words, he gave no indication that he regretted his behavior. She smiled at him nervously.

"I hope you will permit me to make amends for my earlier behavior." He took her hand in his and placed a kiss upon it.

Her smile died. Although his words were clear, his tone was not. "I will permit you to make the attempt, my lord."

He deliberately held her hand a little longer than necessary. She pulled it back as she suddenly recalled the watchful eyes of Mr. McCormack.

A wicked glow lit Mack's face. "Give him a rare trimming, Lady Althea, for he surely deserves one."

"Mack, you imp spawn, you already knew about Lady Althea?" asked the marquess. "And you said nothing to me?" With a friendly malevolence in his voice that hadn't been there in his exchange with her, he threatened his friend, "I'll be even with you, yet."

He turned his attention back to Thea.

"I'm feeling sorely used," he murmured before she could further rake him over the coals. "This noon, your papa gave me a stiff lecture pertaining to the inadvisibility of dallying with his staff. He failed to mention that I'd been dallying with his own daughter."

"Is this your manner of making amends, my lord?" Thea teased. "Are you looking for a scapegoat on which to lay your blame?" She tossed her head playfully. All of a sudden, like the winding down of a clock, her laugh faded into silence. At the door stood Charles with Emma's hand snugly tucked in the crook of his arm.

The color in Thea's cheeks fled. Charles looked at her with a disapproving frown, his eyes scouring over the gentlemen near her. But Thea's eyes were on Emma, who wore a Madonna-like smile. *Were they now betrothed?*

The bustling activity at the door continued as the footman trumpeted the arrival of their dinner guests. Squire Septimus Fossbinder came forward in avid discussion with Emma's father, the Reverend Mr. Rawlings. They were followed by their respective spouses as well as Charles' sister, Jane. By the closed expression on that young woman's face, it was apparent that Jane and the squire were at odds again. Much to the squire's dismay, Jane, at sixteen, was well on her way to becoming bookish. In a few years, she would likely be a thorough bluestocking. And the squire heartily disapproved of any lady's interest in subjects other than those of hearth and home.

Hart had been pleased over his placement beside Lady Althea, the better to ensure that she did penance for her share in this farce. Upon reflection, it was rather amusing that he'd made such an outrageous offer to a chaste and virtuous nobleman's daughter, even if her kiss remained etched within his memory.

Tonight she had dressed demurely in a rose-colored silk gown, with creamy ribbons accenting her coppery hair and tied just above her trim waist. A matching parure of semiprecious stones encircled her wrist and neck. All in all, she was the perfect image of a marriage-mart miss. Definitely not the type of woman with whom he wished to become entangled. So why did the blood pound in his veins whenever she was near?

However could he have believed her a lightskirt? The idea was so foolish as to make him doubt his sanity. However, the earl's earlier comments about his daughter had led Hart to believe her a very young girl. He'd never considered the possibility that Thea and Steyne's little dumpling, Lady Althea, could be one and the same. Lady Althea was no schoolroom miss.

His eyes narrowed as a new thought occurred to him. Had she thought to trap him in a compromising situation? Far sharper ladies than she had tried and failed. This little minx could be trouble. He dismissed the niggling thought that the only trouble thus far had been created by his own fantasy.

Accordingly, he was most attentive to her throughout dinner, making certain she was offered the choicest meats and fruit. She'd not responded to much before the announcement by Squire Fossbinder of the betrothal of his son to Miss Rawlings.

From that moment, Lady Althea's behavior had changed. She'd ignored him before, now she devoted lavish attention on him. Was she attempting to make Mr. Fossbinder jealous? There was some history here and he resolved to learn all he could of the matter.

Until the opportunity presented itself, he relaxed and leaned back to enjoy her attentions.

She was a cunning minx, flirting outrageously with him like the most experienced of London coquettes while peeping at Mr. Fossbinder to check his reaction. In return, that gentleman directed scowls at each of them. Hart bit back a laugh. What a marvelous triangle it was. Yes, he'd have to learn more.

After dinner, Miss Mimms signaled it was time for the ladies to leave the table.

During the interval over port, Mr. Fossbinder continued to glare at him. Blessedly soon, Steyne suggested joining the ladies in the music room and Hart willingly complied.

The music room was large enough to comfortably hold far more than their number. At the head of the room sat a spinet with chairs scattered nearby. Steyne prevailed upon Miss Mimms to play.

Squire Fossbinder called out, in an overly jovial voice, "Too bad Lady Althea cannot carry a tune, Steyne. I'm certain that my future daughter will happily remedy the situation. Emma, won't you honor us with a song or two?"

Miss Rawlings colored then directed a timorous glance at Lady Althea, who waved her on. She made her way to the spinet and Hart's heart sank. Could a night ever be more dull? Some milk-and-water miss caroling them with songs he'd rather forget?

He had to admit, though, that Miss Mimms was a talented pianist and she played simple country airs that Miss Rawlings could easily sing. From the corner of his eye, he noticed Lady Althea placing a hand to her forehead. He grinned. Perhaps she was a bit cast away. He watched as she slipped through the curtains which hid glass-paned doors opening out on the grounds.

After quickly pouring two cups of tea, he turned to join her. Just ahead, he spied Mr. Fossbinder. exit as well. More and more interesting. As unobtrusively as possible, he made for the game room, which had a door leading out onto the same terrace. Balancing the teacups, he quietly slipped outside.

It took a moment for his eyes to adjust as clouds hindered the moonlight. He heard Mr. Fossbinder say, "I know you will wish me happy, Thea."

Hart found himself scowling when Fossbinder took her hands. His scowl became more intense at Lady Althea's reply. "But will you be happy with this? With Emma?"

"I know you wish it could be otherwise," answered Fossbinder with what Hart considered a melodramatic air. "But, Thea, it cannot be. It never was my intention to hurt you, for in hurting you, I've irrevocably hurt myself."

When the gentleman dropped her hand to tick points off on his fingers, Hart could see Thea's shocked expression. "Emma is a most suitable girl. She is sweet and compliant. Our match is all I could wish for. Her portion coupled with my own will set us up in comfort, though not luxury. She will be a good and useful farmer's wife. I am fortunate she will have me."

Hart grinned. She'd expected lovemaking and instead was getting a lesson. Whatever could she see in such a dolt?

Thea grabbed the dolt's arms and shook them. "Oh, Charles, I'm so unhappy. Papa said I would be a dreadful farmer's wife but there is nothing I wish more to be. I've always believed we had an understanding."

"I hope you can forgive me, Thea. I never meant to lead you on. My heart lies heavy in my bosom over my actions this day. My decision was forced upon me and I hope that someday you'll find it in your too-generous heart to forgive me. It is not within my power to support you in the proper manner, in the comfort and consequence you now enjoy. Therefore, I cannot ask that you be my wife."

"Comfort, luxury, consequence!" Thea stormed. "I've heard enough of those words from you and Papa. Can't you see that I have such regard for you?" She threw her arms about his neck and it was all Hart could do to keep himself from separating them. He was surprised by his reaction but Fossbinder had no business being out here with Lady Althea, not since his betrothal had been announced just this evening.

Fossbinder stepped out of her embrace, saving his hide, for Hart would have happily injured him otherwise.

"Wish me happy. And accept my sincerest apologies, Thea. Though it breaks my heart, we must behave with honor," commanded Fossbinder. Hart clenched his fists.

"I wish you happy, Charles," Thea whispered. "You and Emma."

As the object of Thea's affection silently slipped through the large glass doors back into the house, Hart saw a single tear waver at the corner of her eye. Perhaps he *would* damage the bounder after all.

He stepped forward to join her, wanting to offer sympathy. The clouds lifted and clear moonlight illuminated her features.

She dabbed at her eyes. "Have I to add eavesdropping to the list of misdeeds of the dastardly marquess?"

"It's possible. However, the list is quite extensive already." He intently examined her face. "Is that what you call me? The dastardly marquess?"

Thea's only answer was a shrug and a languorous smile.

"Why am I not surprised?" Hart asked and shook his head. "I thought you might be needing some tea." He indicated the cups in his hands, then gave her one and watched with raised brows as she drained the glass. "Do you mind my company, Thea?"

The beverage seemed to lift her mood somewhat, but she appeared either unable or disinclined to speak. Hart emptied his own cup then took hers and placed it upon a stone balustrade.

The spinet's soft refrains could be heard but Miss Rawlings was no longer singing. The night was balmy and a gentle wind nipped at the hem of Lady Althea's gown. Stars twinkled mysteriously and the beautiful three-quarter moon shone down upon them. The chirp of crickets accentuated the melodies of Miss Mimms' waltz. Thea swayed softly to the music.

Taking this as a cue, Hart took her hand in his and settled his other hand against her back. She shivered at his touch but allowed him to draw her into the dance.

Thea's skin glowed with a pearl-like hue. Hart felt his mouth go dry. He dampened his lips and swallowed. Her hand was petal-soft against his own. A desire to kiss her seized him.

He stopped dancing and pulled her a step closer, completely into his arms. Framing her face with his hands, he used his thumbs to tilt her chin upwards. He slowly lowered his lips to meet hers. "Now, Thea, my reward."

He was astounded. When he'd seen Thea in Fossbinder's arms, he'd felt angry and disillusioned. Yet now, he felt possessive of her, as if she was his responsibility to look after. The fact was, she confused him. His plan called for teaching her that teasing a gentleman the way she had him could ricochet. And now he was the one suffering from the backlash. What was she doing to him?

Was Steyne Hall enchanted, disordering the wits of all who resided within? How could he feel so possessive of a girl he hardly knew? And how could he desire an innocent the way he did her?

Now he was holding her within his arms. It broke all the rules of propriety but somehow it didn't feel wrong. Her response told him Thea was an innocent, a child in a woman's body. That odd mixture of purity and passion gave his desire an additional edge, a need to protect her. She was sweet, so sweet.

Hart broke the kiss, not because he wanted to but because honor required it.

"You're not stopping, my lord?" Thea slowly opened her eyes and he noticed her pupils were widely dilated and her lips swollen.

"Oh, Thea." He kissed the tip of her nose. "Do you really wish for more?"

Wicked green eyes glinted at him and then retreated behind closed lids. "Yes, please, my lord," she replied and raised her face to him.

"Do you not feel that it is time to drop the 'my lord's'?"

"Then shall I call you by your full title, *my lord*?" Thea's lashes flew open and she pressed her mouth to his.

"You cat," he whispered with a gurgle. "You will call me Hart."

"Yes, Hart." She sighed his name and he could withstand no more. She'd done it to him again. Groaning, he caught her lips to his. It took all of his willpower to gentle the kiss and pull away.

She murmured, "The music has stopped."

"Um, yes." Hart stood looking into her eyes, then shook his head from side to side. "No, I hear it yet." He kissed her once more, then hoping to reach safety, he hurried her back into the music room.

It was empty.

Chapter Five

"Thea." That settled it. The empty room spoke volumes. The guests had all departed and she was well and truly compromised. Hart tugged her back into his arms.

Being in his arms was comforting but Thea knew she'd have to say it. Aware her plan had misfired, she could sense he was about to speak of marriage and she would not marry him, a man who did not love her. "You must not speak to Papa."

Through gritted teeth he asked, "Thea, why must I not speak with your father?"

"I—I enjoyed our kiss, but . . ."

"But?" He prompted her.

"It was just a kiss."

"Just a kiss? It was not just a kiss. In fact, I must state emphatically, *it was not just a kiss*." Harting-

58

field's face took on a mulish expression. "In any case, if I deem it appropriate to speak with your father, then I will do so."

"You are making this quite difficult, Hart." Thea stepped out of his embrace. Her plan had gone completely awry. "I must be honest with you. I hoped to give you a distaste for me. I was being wanton."

"No, you weren't."

"I mean, I was attempting to be wanton."

He gave her a distracted look. "You were being. . . wanton?"

"Yes." Thea stood her ground.

Lord Hartingfield looked deeply into her eyes. His face hardened. "To trap me into marriage," he finally replied.

"To make you wish *not* to marry me."

Completely stunned, Hart felt his mouth drop. Considering the legions of young ladies and their mamas who had tried to ensnare him, it never occurred to him that any woman, Thea included, would desire otherwise. Insensibly, it struck him that her kisses, those glorious kisses might have been an act?

It took all of his considerable self-control to keep his hands from encircling Thea's swanlike neck and squeezing. He reached for her to jolt her into sensibility. Instead, the intended shake metamorphosed into another gentle kiss. "It wasn't totally an act, was it, Thea?"

"No," she gasped.

"There is magic between us. Would it be so unbearable to marry me? You must feel the magic, the rightness as well as I," he coaxed. Then he froze. He could not believe those words had left his mouth. What was he saying? It occurred to him that while he'd had no intention of marrying her, it was of utmost importance to him that Thea desire it.

Yet, it would be dishonorable of him not to marry a young innocent whom he had compromised. "Thea, our actions this night will necessitate marriage."

"My regard belongs to another." She pulled away.

Hart's grip tightened. "Who, that dunderhead farmer?"

"Charles is not a dunderhead! He's wonderful."

"He's so wonderful that he appears to prefer the charms of Miss Rawlings, Thea."

In a sharp gasp, Thea caught her breath. "No, it is merely that he feels the difference in our stations so keenly."

"I, at least, have one thing to thank him for," he intoned as brushed a curl from her eyes.

"What is that?"

"He taught you well."

"Oh!" She flung his hands away.

"You do not deny it, I see," he said caustically.

Thea cried out, "You are impossible, my lord. Charles would never have kissed me in this manner. In fact, he has never kissed me at all." Her gown had been crumpled by his embrace and she extended a hand to smooth it. "Unlike you, Charles is a gentleman."

"Do not try to flummox me."

"It was my second kiss ever. Yesterday you stole the first." Hart heard the distress in her voice as she fought back tears. "You are c–c–cruel, my lord. Miss

Mimms told me I would always remember my first kiss and now, n–n–now I will always remember this!" She turned and fled the music room.

Hart placed a hand to his forehead. What had he done? Why did the girl always make him lose control? Was his own self-importance of such magnitude that a young woman's pride and innocence must be sacrificed? He stared at the doorway through which she had departed then took a seat at the spinet and idly began to pick out the melody of their waltz.

He would speak with Steyne in the morning and hope to atone for his actions by offering for her. As much as he hated the thought of descending into the parson's mousetrap, no other option was open to him. Besides, there would be obvious benefits to marrying her.

The music of the waltz became more pronounced as he played in earnest.

He refused to believe that she loved that—that bag of stuffed feathers called Fossbinder. And Steyne would be delighted to have nabbed such a matrimonial prize for his daughter. Frustrated by these thoughts, his hands came down in a crash upon the ivory keys.

As he entered the hall to make his way upstairs, he heard a noise. He froze and listened intently.

"Pssst."

Lord Steyne peered from his study in hopes of catching Hartingfield. He did not wish to alert the household, most particularly his daughter, to the dialogue he hoped would soon take place between him and the marquess. Just then, he saw the gentleman exit the music room and head toward the stairway. "Pssst."

Hart stopped and rubbed his ear.

"Pssst," Steyne uttered a little more loudly. Hartingfield craned his neck and examined the dimly lit hall. Then his eyes met Steyne's.

He opened his mouth to speak but Steyne shushed him, whispering, "Quiet. She's just gone to the kitchens." Steyne then motioned him to enter the study.

Once Hartingfield crossed the doorway, Steyne firmly closed the door. "Have you compromised her?" he asked in an intentionally conversational tone, on his way to the chair behind his desk.

Hart found a seat in front of the massive desk, but did not meet the earl's gaze. How long had he remained in the empty and darkened music room? Still, he hadn't truly resolved anything. He had hoped to have a night to think matters over before speaking with the earl. "Yes. I lost my head. If it is any consolation, I intended to speak with you in the morning to request an immediate announcement of our betrothal."

"I've spoken with Thea and I will not force her to marry you."

Hartingfield sat upright and shot a steely look at his host. The man had taken leave of his wits! A father was supposed to insist upon marriage if his innocent daughter was compromised. What was the man playing at? And what was it about Steyne Hall that forcibly reminded him of a madhouse? "I did compromise her."

"You are under a misapprehension. I made acceptable excuses to my guests about your disappearance tonight. So, I repeat, you misapprehend." The earl fidgeted in his chair but his voice did not waver. "Since neither Thea nor I assert she was compromised, there the matter rests. She was not compromised."

"I cannot credit that you would fail to protect Lady Althea this way, Steyne." Hart, himself, wanted to protect her. Mayhap the man was insane—or was he himself a prime candidate for Bedlam?

Lord Steyne's fist descended to his desk with a loud thump. "My daughter will marry for love or not marry at all!"

"Are you saying that she doesn't love me?"

The earl's face crumpled. "I do not know. And neither does she. She says not."

"Am I to assume she told you everything that happened?"

"Enough to assure me you would feel she'd been compromised and you would try to force her into an unwanted marriage," the earl replied.

Hart's eyes narrowed. "Surely she did not imply I had forced unwanted attentions upon her?"

"No, merely that one of her schemes had reversed on her." The old earl plucked at his upper lip for a moment. He then reached into his vest and pulled out a letter. Holding out the packet, he said, "Read this."

Hart's temples pounded as he stared for some moments at Steyne's outstretched hand. Finally he took the letter, certain the contents would somehow change everything. As if expecting adders to leap out at him, he cautiously opened it, then recognizing the handwriting of his father, began to read. Upon reaching the section where his own name was linked with Thea's he slowly raised his eyes to meet Steyne's.

"Is Lady Althea aware of this letter?" His tone was deadly.

The earl shook his head. "She is totally unaware of it and I would have her remain that way."

It didn't help that his father sought the match. In fact, it did the reverse. Since the death of his mother, he'd found his father to be arrogant and unapproachable. After reaching the age of majority, his relationship with the duke was strained and Hart's first inclination was to pursue whichever course the duke would most dislike. More recently, Hart fought against that urge and tried to use reason rather than impulse in their dealings.

And this still did not change matters. Thea had been compromised.

Feeling firmly caught in the noose, he tapped the letter and asked, "Did you plan this situation?"

"No. But the duke is correct, Thea is very much like her mother. However, she is a spirited girl and I find it increasingly difficult to check her untoward behavior."

"Ah ha," Hart exclaimed with a mock smile. "So you do admit that your daughter is at fault."

"At fault, possibly. But you alone are the one responsible for the position in which she now finds herself." The earl's voice became a shout. "God's blood, man, what were you thinking of, remaining out in the gardens with her beyond all that is proper? I can only assume it was your intent to compromise her!"

Hart had the grace to look ashamed, for Steyne's words held a grain of truth. Some insanity had prompted him to choose just that. Was it his fault that his brain ceased functioning whenever she was near?

Steyne continued, "It is time for her to marry. To that end, it is my plan to send her to London for the season. Her aunt, Lady Prunella, will handle her presentation at court and to society." The older man paused, searching for words. "What I am trying to tell you, Hartingfield, is that I would be delighted by an alliance of our families. I merely will not compel Thea to wed where her heart does not lead her. Therefore, I expect you will do whatever it takes to convince her that you are her choice. Do I make myself clear?"

"You are *directing* that, in London, I court her?" Hart detected the subtle demand behind the earl's words. He did not respond well to demands, subtle or otherwise.

"Yes, unless you are the sort of *gentleman* who preys upon innocent young females. Yes. In London I expect you to court her."

At these words, Hart felt the noose make a final adjustment, almost cutting off his air. Without thought, his hand reached up and pulled at his neckcloth, completely disarranging its once precise folds.

The earl went on, "I'm too old to stand by and watch. While I will not force Thea to marry you, I have insisted she allow you to court her as she would with any of her other suitors. Make your case in London." He stood and placed a crinkled hand on Hart's shoulder. "You are a good lad and I foresee that soon I may call you son. I bid you goodnight."

Hart closed his eyes but heard the earl's footsteps

as he left the room. He sympathized with Steyne, he truly did. Lady Althea wasn't an easy young woman to contain, but he failed to see why he should be elected the one to control her.

Using a neatly folded handkerchief, he wiped perspiration from his forehead. What crazy betwaddled impulse had led him to behave in a manner so depraved?

Of one thing only was he certain. He desired Thea. Wisdom dictated that he avoid her at all costs. After all, his life was pleasant and orderly as it was. The sameness had led to a bit of boredom, but what was boredom compared to sheer madness?

Yet, honor dictated the opposite. And, he was a man of honor.

Making matters worse, he was unable to remove her image from his mind or the feel of her soft skin from his fingertips. As a substitute, a goodly portion of blue ruin would have to suffice. Perhaps a servant would know where some could be obtained.

After yanking the bell-pull, it was only a matter of minutes before a footman responded.

Tearing off his neckcloth, Hart eyed the footman. Then, with a grin, he said, "I'll wager a gold sovereign you can't find me a bottle of gin."

"I'll take you up on that wager, your lordship," the footman agreed and ran to do his bidding before Hart changed his mind.

He was left alone, stroking his ear and muttering to the closed door. "I can only hope the fellow was not another of these cursed phantoms."

* * *

The housekeeper's parlor was nearly dark; blinds prevented all but the dimmest of daylight from entering the room. It was furnished with only the most utilitarian of furniture, not because ornaments were forbidden but because it was simply her character. She stood, bent over the only other occupant of the parlor.

Lady Althea's abigail, Meg, sat pitifully huddled upon a straight-backed chair. She pulled her apron over her head and began to weep in earnest, but not before the housekeeper had seen the red spots covering her tear-streaked face.

"Merciful Heavens," she cried. "Measles!" The housekeeper scurried to summon Miss Mimms.

As his valet placed a tray in front of him, Hart awoke to the muffled sounds of frantic activity at Steyne Hall. Remembrance hit him painfully over the head. His assault upon Lady Althea and his decision to marry the chit had surely been insanity. He wondered if moonlight madness had affected him last evening, or Steyne Hall enchantment? At last he put his disturbing behavior to rest under a heading neatly labeled *overly tired*.

He slurped a bit of his tea and then cringed. How was it possible to sip too loudly? Turning to look over his shoulder at Hobbs, he abruptly checked his movement and placed a hand upon his forehead to make sure it remained attached. "It is time we depart this topsy-turvy household and return to the safety of London."

"I knew you'd come to your senses, m'lord. And, I doubt, none too soon."

Soon, the morning's rituals were complete and Hart, with only a lingering headache, went to inform his host that he would be leaving that noon. Upon hearing Hartingfield's regrets, Steyne had the appearance of a man relieved of a heavy burden. Unknowingly, Hartingfield's eyebrow quirked, the exact image of his father the duke at his stodgy best.

The earl reacted to his arrogant expression, as if the younger man now commanded a higher status. "I hope you will indulge me, Lord Hartingfield, in a request that I will make."

Hart noted the formality of Steyne's speech and studied the man for a clue to his behavior. He had never before noticed just what a booming voice the man had. Could he be regretting his earlier dismissal of his request for Lady Althea's hand? "I will do my best to assist you, sir."

"Thea's abigail has come down with the measles. Miss Mimms reminds me that my daughter has never contracted this ailment." Steyne was aware that he was exaggerating it a bit, but no one knew for certain whether she had ever contracted the disease.

Hart groaned inwardly. Blast it, he knew what would be coming next.

Steyne fidgeted in his chair. "I would be most grateful if you would escort my daughter to her aunt's in London. My original plan was for this to take place in a fortnight though I've been dreading it. I have a great dislike of travel. Miss Rawlings and her nurse were to accompany us since Miss Mimms is scheduled to visit our cousin, Constance. I know it's a great imposition, but I would very much appreciate your assistance in escorting them in my stead."

Though he wanted to court Thea, Hart would have chosen a better time to do it. However, there was only one response he could make. "I would be honored to serve you in this way."

Hart's chagrin at the request was preempted by the large smile that now covered the earl's face.

"We still have other, unfinished, business, sir," Hart said. Failing to discuss this subject would be unacceptable to his own demanding father.

"The seed drill?"

"No, Mack can remain with you to finish the installation. I wished to remind you of the land the duke mentioned in his letter. It adjoins our Haversham estate. He may have used it as an excuse to send me to you but he truly hoped to acquire the property."

The earl took a moment to think. "Shall we consider it a part of Thea's dowry?"

Hart couldn't suppress a self-satisfied smirk. He suspected what was to follow: an acceptance of his offer for Thea. As if his thoughts conjured her up, she burst into the room. She looked most becomingly furious.

"Papa!" Injured rage caused her voice to crack. "I came to ask about your decision to remove me to London. But, did I hear you properly? You are discussing my portion with Lord Hartingfield?"

She turned to face Hart. "Excuse me, my lord. I would speak with my father privately," she said dismissively.

"Althea!" The earl's voice reverberated.

"That is all right, Steyne," he soothed. "I believe *we* understand each other. I must see to my carriage." He nodded to each before leaving the room, causing his head to ache in earnest.

"Papa!" Thea was nearly hopping with anger. "What does this mean? Last evening you promised I should not be forced to wed against my will!"

"Perhaps that promise should be retracted in light of your hoydenish, nay, vixenish behavior, Thea. How could you be so discourteous to a guest in our home?"

"Please forgive me, Papa, but I must have an answer. Have you promised my hand to Lord Hartingfield?"

"With your conduct, you will be fortunate indeed if anyone were to offer for you, my girl, much less someone so well set up as Lord Hartingfield." The earl ran a frustrated palm over his forehead. "Do you think you can attach a gentleman with such ungovernable demeanor?"

"Do you imply that he failed to offer for me?" Her voice was hallow with trepidation. Had she made a fool of herself once again?

"I am implying nothing, Thea. I've sent a message to Emma Rawlings and her nurse to be ready to accompany you to London at noon today. You'll want to make ready as well. Lord Hartingfield graciously offered his escort, and I sincerely pity the man."

Chapter Six

"I'm afraid you'll have to travel ahead with Mack and the luggage, Hobbs." Hart heard the thumps of frenzied employment seeping through the thick walls of the stately home. His bedchamber now looked barren, as if the removal of his possessions had stripped it of its essence. Hobbs stood by his side, sealing the final trunk.

"You're not tryin' to tip me the wink, are you, my lord?" Suspicion sharpened Hobbs' face.

"No, I wish it were that simple." Hart cringed when he heard a particularly loud bang coming from the ceiling directly over head. "I will not be traveling alone." He walked over to the window to glance at the weather outside. It was a typically gray English day. Although the sun was visible, it struggled with

71

overcast skies for supremacy and there was a decided nip in the air. Another boring day for travel.

"You mean—you can't mean the chit's agreed to be your wife? Not an earl's daughter."

"No." Hartingfield slashed at his thigh with leather riding gloves. "I am escorting her to London."

Hobbs looked at him in astonishment. "Ye won't be wedding her?"

"Last night I came within inches of cupid's bow-string, Hobbs. The minx wouldn't have me."

"No female in her right mind would turn you down."

"Lady Althea did." Hart studied his nails. "Perhaps you have the right of it. Mayhap her wits have gone begging. However, I fully intend that she *shall* be my wife."

Hart walked over to a chair and took a seat. "I'll escort her to Lady Prunella's and use the time in transit in an attempt to alter her decision."

Hobbs shot him a quizzical look. "Are you certain you won't be needing me?"

"Not this time," replied Hart with a glint of laughter in his eye. "We will be accompanied by her companion, so I won't require your service as duenna." More seriously, he added, "By tomorrow or the next day at latest, I hope to be in London. You may travel ahead without concern to assure my comfort when I arrive."

The luggage carriage left at noon. Thea had already bid farewell to Uncle Egbert as well as the staff at Steyne. With tear-filled eyes, she turned to her father.

"Oh, Papa. I shall miss you dreadfully. Are you certain that you cannot accompany me?"

"No, m'dear. Ever since Caroline . . ." The old earl's voice trailed off.

Thea bowed her head. She remembered too well how devastated her father had been after the death of her mother. Her parents had left that morning, in high spirits over their planned trip to London. Their carriage had overturned, killing her mother immediately and leaving her father desolate.

"I am not at all sure that sending you to your aunt's is the right thing to do, Thea. Mayhap you would be better off remaining with me, here at Steyne Hall."

"No, Papa. You were correct." She had reconciled herself to the unwanted journey by thoughts of helping her father rid himself of his obsessive fear of travel. Now, Lord Hartingfield would be escorting her. But she retained hopes of luring her father to London, just the same. A wind came up, bellowing her skirts, and for added warmth she pulled at the lapels of her traveling pelisse.

"A London Season is exactly what I need." So saying, she gripped him in a frantic embrace. "Take care of yourself, Papa, and remember, I expect you to come in time for my ball."

If she could get him to London, this once, then perhaps he'd have a chance to heal the nine-year-old wound. Since her mother's death, he'd refused to leave the boundaries of Steyne. This could not be considered healthy for such a previously vibrant man.

Hartingfield stepped forward, blocking her view of the only life she knew, and handed her into the carriage. Emma and her nurse, Mrs. Wiggins, were already settled within.

He faced the earl. "Don't worry, sir. I shall take excellent care of your daughter."

"I know you will." Steyne darted a nervous glance at the coach. "Don't allow the coachman to spring those high-blooded wheelers of yours." His voice turned to a growl. "Remember, if anything happens to my Thea, I'll have your skin."

Steyne schooled the emotion from his face as he turned back to Thea, who leaned through the open carriage window.

"Althea, before your departure, I am hoping you can enlighten me pertaining to a small mystery." He grinned. "There is a blue ribbon collar adorning one of my prize piglets this morning. Can you explain it?"

The traveling carriage was emblazoned with his father's coat of arms. Although the marquess' servants were adorned with the brightly colored blue and silver livery belonging to the Cavendar family, at least he didn't have outriders carrying his banners, as his father's consequence insisted that he use. Hart generally preferred a faster, although less luxurious, method of travel, yet had bowed to the duke's decision that the ancient equipage was called for on this visit to the earl. Thankfully, the coach was roomy and comfortable.

Hart could not sleep and, as expected, the scenery failed to hold his interest. Seeking some diversion, he studied his traveling companions.

Thea was curled up quite like a kitten on the seat opposite him, sound asleep. She wore a pelisse of kings blue, trimmed with narrow fur edges, opened to reveal a yellow muslin traveling gown. Her yellow straw poke bonnet framed her face with several coquettish blue feathers peeking at him, reminding him of the peacock plumes of a few nights earlier.

Miss Rawlings sat beside her to his left, quietly looking out at the scenery. Mrs. Wiggins sat next to him. Since entering the carriage, she'd never said one word. A tedious journey indeed.

He turned his attention back to Thea. Looking at her sweet smile, he recalled the softness of her lips upon meeting his touch. His stomach clenched.

He'd convinced himself that his behavior had been prompted by the lack of sleep. It now appeared, though, that her mere presence affected his wits in some manner. Having seen her in rapt conversation with Miss Rawlings, he'd come to the conclusion that she was young—far too young for him. Who would ever believe he could be totally spellbound by a young miss barely out of the schoolroom? It was simply that he'd been alone for too long.

Once they reached London, he'd soon resolve the matter. Honor dictated that he marry her and marry her he would.

Was he not the most logical of men? Was he not the most dispassionate? Numerous wagers had been entered into the book at White's over when he'd finally lose his head, but never had anyone been so disguised as to suggest a woman as his nemesis. They'd all assumed, as had he, that no woman could ever have such power over him.

And that was correct. Thea had no more influence with him than a servant would. Yes, he'd carry out his agreement to court her. It was his choice to behave honorably. It wasn't because he couldn't do otherwise. He quickly dismissed the thought that anything other than honor was on the line.

It was merely that she'd make a suitable marchioness. Nothing more. Nothing less. The way she crinkled her nose at him had nothing to do with it. The endearing way she'd practically ordered him from Steyne's study had nothing to do with it.

He turned his head and looked out the carriage window. No, he merely acted according to the dictates of society.

Expecting another day of torture, Hart entered the sitting room at the inn set aside for their meals only to find Thea already seated there. She was alone. Neither Emma nor Mrs. Wiggins was in sight.

Now that he had her alone, perhaps he could convince her that a long and tedious courtship would be unnecessary. "Good morning, Thea," he said as he grasped her hand and gently kissed it.

Thea's eyes widened. "Good morning, Lord Hartingfield."

"Hart."

Why was he looking at her so intently, Thea wondered. He cocked his brow and again she felt herself blush. Then he turned her wrist and brushed his lips against the pulse point, and though for a instant she longed to allow him the familiarity, she promptly pulled her hand from his.

"You do not care for my version of breakfast?"

Half scandalized, she repeated, "Breakfast?"

He leaned over her and took a quick taste of her lips. "Yes. A kiss in the morning is my idea of the proper way to break one's fast."

Thea placed her fingers over her lips and watched warily as Hart grinned at her then took a seat. Tension filled the air. To lighten it, she tilted her head and said, "At times you are a charming young boy, Hart, and what woman can resist such appeal?"

"I hope you will soon come around to my way of thinking. But so far, you have been able to do so."

"So far," she agreed dryly.

Hartingfield grinned wickedly. "Are you issuing a challenge?" He rose from his chair, knelt beside her, then swiftly claimed a kiss.

Thea pulled away as if stung.

"No more breakfast?" he asked.

Thea bent forward to pick up her shawl, then wrapped it about her shoulders. "I don't know you well, Hart, but I well know of your reputation as a rake."

"I feel I know you well already." Hart's eyes twinkled as he added, "But I look forward to becoming better acquainted."

"May I have your word this will not happen again?" She meant no more stolen kisses and he knew it.

"The word of a rake, Thea?"

She nodded.

"Very well. You have my word that while we are en route to London, I will not attempt to claim another kiss."

"And afterwards," was her curt rejoinder.

"No." Hart shook his head. "I give you the pledge that I can. After we leave this place, you will have to look after your own interests, for I cannot promise further."

"Well, if you want my company you will need to make the attempt, m'lord."

He turned away to hide his self-disgust that he wasn't able to offer the promise she asked of him. Perhaps she was right. Perhaps he was nothing more than a rake.

"And, Hart?" Thea asked.

"Hmm?"

"I very much enjoyed breakfast."

She had done it to him again.

As the day progressed, only the thought of reaching London the following day kept Thea from leaping from the carriage. Hartingfield winked and blew mock kisses at her in a most annoying manner whenever he thought Emma and Mrs. Wiggins weren't looking. He wasn't always successful at hiding it, though. At one point, Emma had broken into giggles and only a stern look from Thea had silenced her.

That night, Hartingfield arranged for their supper in a private parlor. But this time, she made certain to have both Emma and Mrs. Wiggins beside her when she entered the room.

Hartingfield had been busy. The furniture had obviously been rearranged to provide a cozy dinner table in front of a gently smoldering fire. The only other light was provided by the lone branch of candles decorating the table. When Hart caught her eye and gave her a soulful look, she found herself backing out of the room.

"Good evening, ladies. I took the liberty of ordering dinner." Hart stepped forward to drag her by the arm and led her to a chair. "I hope you will be pleased with what I selected, although I fear our host's cook will not be up to Steyne Hall's standards."

As he seated her, his hand softly grazed her arm in a lover-like gesture. Thea stiffened and pulled away. "Thank you." She heard him chuckle as he circled the table to seat the others.

Both Mrs. Wiggins and Thea's friend, soon to be her former friend if she did not stop encouraging Hart, smiled at him as if enraptured. Thea glared at Emma, who immediately removed all expression from her face. As Miss Mimms had often said, rakes could be most charming. She watched in disdain as Hart charmed both her companions. How could he? And how could they?

After taking a chair beside Thea, Hart reached out to a side table and lifted a bottle.

She watched as he filled their glasses and handed one to each of them. He raised his goblet and took a sip.

"It's a pity." Hartingfield grimaced.

"Has it turned sour?" asked Mrs. Wiggins.

Hart shook his head.

"Is it a poor vintage, Lord Hartingfield?" asked Emma, looking down at her goblet as if it contained dirty water.

Again he shook his head. Then he gazed directly at Thea and said, "It is a pity that no nectar can be as sweet as you."

Mrs. Wiggins gasped and Emma chortled with glee.

Thea couldn't believe he would do this to her. Had he no shame? It was bad enough when they were alone, but for all the world to hear? Underneath the table, she swung out her foot in a mighty kick, then grinned when he hid a cringe of pain. She only regretted that she wore soft slippers rather than a shoe made of sterner material. Steel-tipped might have been a better choice. She'd order some as soon as they reached London. "You seem to forget, my lord, you made me a promise."

"I have no recollection of a promise not to woo you."

"I feel that your vexing behavior is breaking the spirit of your promise."

He wriggled his brows. "That is your just reward for accepting the word of a rake."

"Shall I?" he asked Mrs. Wiggins as he gestured at the dishes of food sitting on the side table. She nodded and he proceeded to load a plate for them. When it came Thea's turn, he filled every available space on it, then offered her the overflowing plate.

She glared at him mulishly, refusing to accept it.

Hart shrugged, then settled the plate in front of her. He filled his own plate. Turning back to her, he wordlessly blew her a kiss before devouring a forkful of chicken.

When Thea still made no move to eat, Hart said, "I will not be the one who goes hungry tonight."

Curse the man, Thea thought, as she gathered up a bite of mutton and chewed on it.

"Marry me, Thea."

This time not only Emma but Mrs. Wiggins as well broke up into laughter.

Thea nearly choked.

The next morning, after a sleepless night spent worrying about her behavior, Thea took tea in her room rather than risk coming across Hart alone. When the hour became quite late, she worried because no one had summoned her to the carriage. In hopes of discovering the cause, she opened her door to peep out. Hart stood not five feet away in the hallway. She quickly slammed the door, but not before hearing him call out, "Marry me, Thea!" The scoundrel.

A few moments later, there came a tap at the door. Throwing it open, she was prepared to ring a peal over Hart's head. She felt a momentary disappointment when she found Emma standing there.

"May I come in?"

"Please do."

"I overheard Lord Hartingfield speaking with his groom. It appears there will be a slight delay before our departure."

"Whatever caused the delay, I'm grateful for it. I have something important to ask you, Emma." She took her friend's arm and led her to a settee.

"Have you ever given any thought to immoral women, Emma?" Seeing her companion's lost look, Thea continued, "I mean, to what makes them immoral?"

"I can't say that I have. Why?"

"I have begun to wonder if I am fast."

"Whatever have you been up to?" Emma appeared delightfully shocked.

Thea quickly added, "I don't mean that I have yet done anything I shouldn't." At least she hoped she hadn't. "I merely find myself wanting to."

"With—with Lord Hartingfield?" Emma's voice was thick with disbelief. When Thea blushed and nodded, Emma insisted, "Tell me *all*, at once!"

"There isn't really much to tell. He has kissed me." When Thea heard her friend's giggle, she added, shamefacedly, "Twice."

"No, Thea!" Emma's scandalized voice reduced to a whisper, "How could you?"

"It wasn't so much how I could but rather, how I could not. And that is the crux of the matter." Thea paused, giving emphasis to her words. "Since my heart is not involved, I must be fast."

Emma's experience could be summed up with one terribly chaste kiss, given to her by Charles, upon her acceptance of his proposal. She wasn't sure how to advise her friend but did not wish to reveal her own inexperience. She settled on an understanding look.

"I have decided upon a course of action." Thea slashed the air with her hand. "Upon reaching London, I must quickly look over the eligibles and select a husband right away. Surely it cannot take too long to fall in love. Perhaps with marriage, children and a household to distract me, I may avert my baser instincts." She took a quick look at Emma to see how she had taken her impassioned monologue.

Emma glowed with admiration. "What a wonderful solution, Thea. I only wish it had been my own." She patted her companion's arm. "But are you certain you could not come to care for Lord Hartingfield?"

"I cannot see how." Thea bit her lip. "Miss Mimms warned me about men like him. He's a profligate. A cad. He cares more for his cattle than me. Why, I'd rather live my life as an ape leader than tied to him.

"Besides, it is my intent to reside at Steyne and I do not think Lord Hartingfield would agree. I shall be much better off seeking a more compliant gentleman."

"Very well. We can be comfortable again with such a good plan to follow. But, Thea." Emma would die of curiosity if she didn't ask. "I *would* like to hear more about Lord Hartingfield's kisses."

Chapter Seven

London was a teeming, smoke- and people-filled metropolis, greatly exceeding Thea's expectations. The travel-wearied party approached the outskirts of town in the late afternoon. Thea's stomach was aflutter with excitement as the coach made its stately way through narrow city streets still bustling with activity.

Concerned about the necessity of their close proximity, she had felt her burden lighten considerably upon learning of Hart's decision to ride beside the carriage on his own mount. Just then he waved at her and she ducked her head back into the carriage.

Hart acknowledged her need to avoid him, and it did not please him. After all, she had agreed to get to know him and that promise did not signify they would be leg-shackled. But, she *would* make good on her promise. And he *would* do his utmost to convince her of the benefits of their union.

The carriage pulled up to Lady Prunella's elegant town house, a large Georgian structure. He dismounted to help them from the carriage. An elderly and rheumatic butler opened the door and led them into a cavernous hallway replete with Grecian statues.

Mrs. Wiggins would be traveling on to visit with an old friend. After Thea bid her goodbye, Emma gave her a tremendous hug. As they spoke, Hart whispered to Thea, "I will call upon you and your aunt in the morning."

"I thank you for your consideration, my lord, but that will be unnecessary."

"Necessary, or not," he stated with a resolute expression, "I will see you tomorrow. *Au revoir*, my sweet."

Thea watched him depart with Mrs. Wiggins, then turned to the butler.

"My lady is expecting you, Lady Althea, Miss Rawlings," he said. "She requested that you be brought to her upon your arrival."

"Thank you," she replied. "And you are?"

"Phelps, my lady."

Thea nodded.

"Sarah," he flicked his fingers and a maidservant appeared out of nowhere, "will escort you to Lady Prunella." He bowed as the middle-aged servant led them up the curving stairwell.

During the walk through the townhouse, Thea was surprised to see what appeared to be dozens of footmen lining the halls and passageways. She brushed the thought off as tiredness and continued on her way.

Passing along what seemed to be an endless corridor, Emma accidentally dropped her reticule. Both she and Thea were astounded when two extremely lofty footmen dove for it, almost beaming each other on the head. Neither young woman could restrain a laugh at their antics.

The maid had almost lost them, having failed to notice the commotion. The young women rushed to catch up with her.

Another footman swung open the sitting room door and announced their arrival. Upon entering, Thea felt a bit intimidated by the Egyptian furnishings in the room, which even included a gold-leafed daybed in the shape of a crocodile with clawed feet for legs. However, Aunt Prunella's greeting could not have been warmer.

"Welcome, my dears! Thea, I was so delighted to receive your letter about bringing Miss Rawlings with you." Directing a sweet smile at the young woman, she added, "Welcome. I haven't seen either of you in dog's years."

"Yes, Aunt." Thea gave her a quick embrace. "I was fourteen at your last visit to Steyne."

"Oh, no. Can it be that long? Well, no matter. Let me take a look at you both." The older woman pulled out a quizzing glass and eyed Thea carefully. The magnified view of Prunella's fluttering eye made her giggle.

"And, Thea, just look at you! My, you have grown into a beauty. You are absolutely the image of your sweet mother, God rest her soul. She would be so proud of you now."

Turning to Emma, Lady Prunella continued, "And you, Miss Rawlings . . . no, that is too formal, we shall be the best of friends, so might I call you Emma?"

"Certainly, Lady Prunella."

"No, dear. In return you, too, must call me Aunt. You have grown quite lovely, child. Such sweetness."

Aunt Prunella went on with a seemingly endless stream of chatter, punctuating every point she made by gesturing with her fan. Thea stole a look at her friend, amazed by her aunt's animation. This was not her normal manner. What had happened to the lethargic Lady Prunella?

After feeding them a refreshing tea, Aunt Prunella suggested they proceed to their suite of rooms to get some rest. "For you must know, I am having one of my educational salons tonight to discuss the scientific principles of electricity. If you feel quite up to it you may certainly attend. If not, you may take dinner in your suite and we will meet over breakfast tomorrow to discuss how we will go on during your visit."

Heads spinning with weariness, they declined the invitation to attend the salon. Thea murmured that a good sleep was called for. They bid Aunt Prunella goodnight and with a footman's assistance retreated to their suite of rooms.

It contained a cozy sitting room surrounded on each side by a bedroom and dressing room. Fatigue overcame Thea, who sat upon a Sheraton armchair while Emma said, "I'll take the pink bedroom, Thea. You take the blue." Thea agreed happily since blue was her favorite color.

Both rooms were fashionably and generously furnished, each a mirror image of the other except for the color scheme.

Following a soft tap at the door, a young maid entered. With a deep and awkward curtsey, she introduced herself, "I am Jones, m'ladies. The housekeeper, Mrs. Roberts, suggested I act as ladies' maid to you both until your own abigail arrives."

"Thank you, Jones. You may find the job a bit onerous since my abigail is laid up with the measles. If you feel game to the task, you may first help Miss Rawlings and then attend me when you are finished." Thea smiled with friendship at the timid maid.

Jones was heartened by her new lady's condescension. She had heard that these noblemen's daughters were, by and large, terribly haughty. How lovely that it proved to be untrue.

In the breakfast parlor the next morning, Aunt Prunella's voice rang out melodically, "Good morning, my darlings." It was obvious she felt quite sprightly. She allowed Thea and Emma to fill their breakfast plates from the buffet before she continued. "Now, let us get down to business at once."

Thea and Emma each took a seat beside her at the ornate table adorned with large china figurines of a shepherd and shepherdess.

Lady Prunella was an attractive, young-looking woman whose appearance belied her forty-eight years. She was dressed in a light blue morning gown of Bel-

gian lace. Her long sleeves were tightly fitted to her
arms until just beneath the elbows, where they flared
out enormously. The blue flared sleeves were finished
with white embroidered eyelet and the underside was
filled with layer upon layer of white lace. Each time
she moved her arms, the sleeves would billow
dramatically.

Thea glanced down at her own countryfied attire
and realized that it wasn't at all the thing, in spite of
Miss Mimms' attempts to see her properly outfitted.

"Are you here to get some town bronze or to nab
husbands?" Aunt Prunella asked bluntly. Thea gazed
at her in astonishment.

"You must know that they are not the same things
at all." She pointed to Thea and her sleeve swung open
like a fan. "Now, answer my question."

Thea recovered her wits. "Emma is betrothed, Aunt,
to the squire's son at Steyne. And," she paused to take
a deep gulping breath, "I am here to find a husband.
Quickly."

The older woman raised her brows at this comment.
"Quickly, Thea? Do you not feel it is best to take one's
time on these matters?"

"Yes, Aunt." It wouldn't do to have her aunt thinking there was any reason for undue haste. She hurriedly explained, "I merely meant that I eagerly
anticipate the moment when I may bestow my esteem
and affection on the gentleman of my choice."

"Very well, Thea." Lady Prunella silently stared at
her for a moment as if considering the veracity of
her statement. "Now girls, we must make our plans
accordingly.

"There are three areas that must be covered. Appearances, experiences, and strategies. Appearances are the simplest. For both of your objectives, dressing all the crack is essential. I have already made an appointment for you with my modiste, Madame Brandt." She eyed their attire. "You will need morning gowns, evening gowns, full evening gowns, walking dresses, promenade gowns, just to name a few. And you, Thea, will require a court dress for your presentation to Her Majesty, the Queen."

She turned to Emma. "I am sorry, dear, but for this one occasion only, you need be excluded. Otherwise, you will accompany each other everywhere. Luckily your coloring is such that you truly complement the other."

"But the expense!" gasped Emma. Thea opened her mouth to offer financial assistance but Lady Prunella spoke first.

"This will be at my expense, of course. I cannot have it said that I would, in any way, stint my niece and her lovely friend." Her voice took on a stubborn tone. "Therefore, there will be no argument on this point."

"Thank you, Lady Prunella," said Emma, awed by her generosity.

"No more of that." Lady Prunella rapped the girl's knuckles with her fan. "We already determined that I shall be your Aunt as well, Emma.

"I corresponded with Lady Sefton, and received vouchers to Almack's for each of you. Maria was such a dear to send them right over." Lady Prunella waved the packet at them. "After your presentation at court,

Thea, as you know, we shall have a ball to present both of you to society. I am planning a majestic event, I am already conjuring up some splendid ideas. Well, that can come later."

Thea's enthusiasm rose. Everything the older woman said created a richer sense of excitement. What fun they would have!

"I have also arranged for my hair dresser to attend you. Wouldn't you each like to have one of the modish short styles, your heads all in curls?"

"I would love it above all things," replied Emma. But Thea had her doubts.

"Would it be possible to make it more fashionable without cutting it all off, Aunt? Papa adores my long tresses."

"Certainly, dear. Henri will strive to give you whatever look you desire. I may as well tell you now, I have hired a dancing master. You will both wish to be *au courant* with the latest dances. Thea, have you had the opportunity to waltz?"

Thea tried to speak but couldn't utter a word. She, instead, reddened miserably, having recalled just how that dance had ended.

"I can see you have. How about you, Emma? No? Well, let me warn you, no waltzing here in London without the approval of one of the patronesses of Almack's first.

"I think that's enough to begin with. Have you any questions or particular wishes?"

Thea spoke up, "Yes, Aunt. Papa has given me this billet for you." She handed her the thick packet.

Lady Prunella opened it as Thea timidly continued, "Since I am hoping to quickly fall in love and wed, would you be able to give me a list of the more eligible bachelors? I would not wish to waste my time, you see, with fortune hunters and the like."

Aunt Prunella's eyes flashed with approval at this evidence of practicality. "I will provide you with plenty of paper. I suggest you begin a listing of the eligibles whose names I provide you. We must proceed scientifically, with method and intellect."

She opened the billet and discovered a draft upon Drummund's bank, along with a letter of credit. Separating the earl's letter from the balance of the packet, she asked, "Do you know any bachelors in town?"

"Only Lord Hartingfield."

Lady Prunella's eyes narrowed. "Only? The most sought-after bachelor in town and you call him only?" She looked down to scan her brother-in-law's letter.

Thea was amazed. Hart really *was* the "monarch of the peak," as Mimsie had once described him, reinforcing her opinion of him. The fellow was arrogant, demanding and most likely fickle—not at all a suitable candidate for a husband. Men like him were already in love: with themselves.

Aunt Prunella continued reading. "What's this about the measles, Thea? You had them when you were three. In fact, I came to Steyne at the time to help your poor mama."

"I did not remember, Aunt." Drat, if only she had known, she could have avoided the journey with Hart.

"Well, I see how it was. Your Papa would hardly remember since he was on the continent at the time and Miss Mimms, well . . . However, you are here with me now and Lord Hartingfield escorted you."

Emma's next words jolted Thea.

"She has already declined his offers," Emma pointed at Thea with her fork, "but he will not take no for an answer, Aunt Prunella. He cannot truly be the most sought-after bachelor in town?"

Lady Prunella couldn't believe her ears. With widened eyes, she discarded the earl's billet and reached into her reticule, withdrawing a vial of smelling salts. After taking a quick whiff, she turned to Thea and said, "The charmer has fallen for a green girl, just out of the schoolroom, has he? Do not tell me you declined an offer from Lord Hartingfield!"

Thea nodded sheepishly.

"Well, what a man can't have, he simply *must* acquire." The earl's letter made the situation perfectly clear. Lady Prunella looked Thea directly in the eye. "But seriously, Althea, how much higher can you look? The heir to a dukedom! Are you aware of just how many women have set their cap at him? You would be astounded." She nodded. "You are just like your mother, aren't you?"

"I certainly wish to be, ma'am. But what does Mama have to do with Lord Hartingfield?"

"She disobliged her family and declined his father, the Duke of Devonshrop, to marry your father, Thea. That is what she has in common with you."

"I've always known she'd made a love-match. I never knew the exact circumstances. I am proud to think I am like her, Aunt." Thea's face glowed with satisfaction.

"And to think, I did it unknowingly." The light died from her face. "Papa is trying to arrange a marriage of convenience between us. Lord Hartingfield cares nothing for me, therefore I must remain steadfast in my determination to decline his offers. I shall only marry for love . . . like Mama."

"I believe you are making a dreadful mistake, Thea, but perhaps we may turn it to your benefit." Lady Prunella sought a solution that would encourage Hartingfield without frightening her niece. "We must persuade Lord Hartingfield to call often and gad you about as much as possible. Whatever your personal opinion of him, the *ton* considers him the arbiter of fashionable behavior. His attentions will give a decided cachet to your reputation as a diamond of the first water."

Thea's explanation had failed to impress Lady Prunella. With all of England to choose from, Hartingfield would hardly be likely to accept an arranged marriage, especially to a country miss. Although her niece was an extremely wealthy heiress, it was unlikely *that* would sway him in her favor. The only answer she could find was Hartingfield had fallen in love, at long last. Picturing the amazed face of Maria Sefton, Lady Prunella looked forward to the delights which awaited them this most splendid London Season.

"You are looking more youthful than ever, Lady Prunella." Hart brushed his lips against her upraised hand and inwardly cringed when he saw the gilt monstrosity she was seated upon. He looked about the overly ornate Egyptian-styled room in bewilderment. He had requested an interview with Lady Althea and instead had been led here. A room that looked as though some long-dead Egyptian mummy had been sprung back to life and given free hand to redecorate. Where was Thea?

"You Cavendar men were always known as flatterers." Lady Prunella motioned to a chair with her fan. "Please be seated."

Hart adjusted his tall frame into the slender, yet thankfully solid Etruscan chair she indicated.

"Well, young man, aren't you going to ask?"

"Ask?"

"Yes, ask why I have arranged for this tete-a-tete."

"I did not wish to be impertinent, ma'am." Hart steeled himself. Was the woman seeking a verbal sparring match? What had Thea told her?

"No more roundaboutations!" In what appeared to be an attempt to ruffle his calm manner, she took her time pouring two small sherries and slowly handed him one.

She took a ladylike sip of her drink, then jabbed her fan toward him like a rapier and demanded, "Why have you led the child to believe you have no affection for her?"

"What has led you to believe that I have, Madam?" He resented this intrusion into his personal affairs. His knuckles tightened on the crystal sherry glass, threatening to break the delicate stem.

Lady Prunella began to laugh. "Egads, you're like your father, aren't you? He was never one to give anything away." Her eyes turned dreamy. "I must say I always held him in affection, although, since I was in the schoolroom at the time of our acquaintance, he much preferred the attractions of my older sister, Thea's mother." She made a small grimace and broke off the conversation momentarily to fiddle with her fan.

"I wish to see my niece happily settled, and it is my belief that you are uniquely qualified to assure her happiness." Lady Prunella stood, signaling him to remain seated, and began to pace. "Thea is determined, like her mother before her, to form a love-match. Surely it is within the powers of someone so accomplished to allow the child to believe that you are truly smitten?"

Thoroughly uncomfortable with the tenor of the conversation, he asked in a frigid voice, "You would have me mislead her?"

"Absolutely not!" She stopped and clasped the arm of his chair. "You have compromised the girl in her father's home! And, from what intuition tells me, not once, but several times over. Your repeated actions lead one to believe that you have either thrown away all your gentlemanly principles or have, at long last, fallen in love. Had you not realized that your determined pursuit of Thea implies that you have found your nemesis at last?"

Had he not used that very word to himself? *Nemesis.* Perhaps it was more than desire for Thea's physical attractions that had prompted his actions. But why should he admit such a fatal weakness to the girl's relation? "I find myself drawn to her, certainly. But to imply that there is anything other than an . . . attraction?" He shrugged his shoulders. If he said it often enough, perhaps he could convince himself.

"If you would only make yourself more approachable."

Hart's brow cocked. "Approachable? I am the very soul of approachable. You must have me confused with my father."

"Hah! If you are so approachable then why is Thea this moment composing a list of eligible bachelors? Advances do not make one approachable. Thea is a sweet and uncorrupted young lady. Instead, your importunities have, understandably, scared her half out of her senses."

It was possible Lady Prunella was entirely correct, but Hart was not yet ready to admit it. "I have been the most reasonable and patient of gentlemen, ma'am. I have never, and will never, push Thea beyond the bounds with which she is comfortable."

"Enough of this nonsense." She returned to the couch, having finally reached the end of the margin that she'd granted him. The young man was angry rather than feeling the gratitude she had hoped for. She took a seat. "You *will* agree to squire her about?"

Hart nodded, but betrayed no further emotion.

"Do you plan to continue pressing your suit?"

"I've had little success thus far, ma'am. What would you have me do?"

"Stick with it, young man! In light of your previous rakish behavior toward the chit, the least you can do is persevere. If you will stop frightening the child, I assure you, Thea will come around to the idea that you are the man for her."

"Might I see her now?" Hart asked through clenched teeth. He didn't want to deal with this.

"You're very much like your father." Lady Prunella sighed and jerked the bell-pull.

The door flew open.

Chapter Eight

"**S**o you did come," accused Thea as she entered and spotted Lord Hartingfield. Their eyes met in silent skirmish, as if each willed the other to back down or come out full force in open warfare.

Thea backed down first. She turned to Lady Prunella and asked, "You wished to see me, Aunt?"

"Yes, Lord Hartingfield has graciously offered to take you for a carriage drive through the park today."

Thea's horrified expression spoke volumes, and the older woman added, "Emma might wish to accompany you."

He didn't miss the little vixen's smile of victory at hearing these words. Well, they would see who won *this* round. "I need to speak with Lady Althea. Alone."

Lady Prunella cast him an assessing look. "Very well, you have five minutes and the door must remain open." She left the room without a backward glance.

Hart gave Thea a stony smile. She looked as if she'd rather take a swim in the Thames than face these few moments alone with him.

But, he wanted the issue resolved. The tedium of courtship could be avoided as well as the type of scene in which he'd just participated, if only she would agree to an immediate announcement.

"You rashly refused my offer, Thea. Now that you have had time to reconsider, I intend to have the banns read without delay."

"My decision remains unchanged." She raised her chin.

Hart closed the space between them and tenderly placed his palm against her cheek. "Marry me, Thea." He rubbed his fingers across her lips. "Shall I persuade you to reconsider?"

"No. You cannot."

"Do you *truly* doubt my ability to do so? Don't." He brought his lips to hers in a gentle kiss.

He felt her body stiffen. "You will have to do better than that, my lord."

"I suspect if I had a little more time available to me, Thea, you would welcome my advances."

"Of all the arrogance," she spat back at him. "As if time spent in your presence would alter my decision in any way."

"*Will you, nill you, I will marry you,*" he quoted, for this hellcat did remind him of that fateful Kate. Yet, he hadn't intended to make such a threat. How could he convince her and yet remain a gentleman?

What had happened to his usual aplomb? And, what had him acting such a nodcock?

He noticed that her hands were trembling. Lady Prunella's warnings came back to him and he released her. He felt as though a jolt of lightning struck and he finally admitted the truth to himself.

Lady Prunella had been completely correct. He *was* in love with the saucy chit, and, in the eye-opening moment, he realized his advances did frighten her.

He wanted to make an apology, to start anew, but Thea stopped him, saying, "In the future, my lord, I will not permit you to be alone with me."

Their argument was doomed to remain unresolved, for they were interrupted.

"How do you do, my lord?" Emma Rawlings stood in the open doorway. As if sensing the strained atmosphere, she announced, "Thea, if you mean to drive with Lord Hartingfield, you need to change your attire."

Hart was not yet ready to reveal his weakness to Thea. He looked the hellion directly in her eyes. If he had fallen in love so easily, it was possible that he'd fall out of love just as effortlessly. He needed time to think. "My apologies, Lady Althea, I recollect a previous engagement for this afternoon. Perhaps we may schedule our drive for another time?"

Over the next several days, Thea and Emma became quite friendly with their maid, Jones. One morning while Jones prepared a bath for her new mistress, Thea brought up her papa's prize pigs.

"Oh, mum, I hate to gainsay you, but," the young maid twisted her apron with her hands, "my intended is a swine breeder. His piggery is considered the most superior in all of England! Why, just last week, he took the prize at our county fair. This week, he is competing against prize-winning pigs from three counties. And, he is a cert to win."

"How interesting."

"Yes'm. Why, jest ask anybody from High Wycombe, and they'll all tell you, Robert Tate's pigs be the best!" Jones added some sweet-smelling salts to the water.

"Papa would be delighted if I could aid him in his dream to produce the finest pigs in England." Thea paused to shake out her curls in preparation for her bath. "Would your intended consider selling one or two piglets?"

"Happen he may say yes, though twouldn't be usual-like, m'lady." She arose to help Lady Althea with her buttons. "Since we are trying to put by the monies to set up house, and seeing as how I do for you and all, I am cert he would be happy to oblige, ma'am."

"Then we must attend this fair. When and where is it to be held?"

The very next morning found the two young women seated upon a gig, a groom driving them out of London proper. Emma had declined Thea's invitation to accompany them and instead said she would enjoy some time spent at Hatchard's, selecting an engrossing book. Therefore, Thea, dressed in one of her old country gowns and, Jones, wearing her very best, decided to make a day of it.

It was a relief to escape the rules and doctrines that young ladies had to obey in town, and an added inducement was some fresh country air. Thea threw back her head and took a deep breath. With each step of the horse's hooves, her spirits climbed higher.

As they arrived in the country town, she noted it was congested with farmers and tradesmen selling their wares. There were stalls with merchants selling many different beverages including ginger beer, lemonade, peppermint water, coffee, cocoa and tea. Other stalls sold hot and cold foods, sweets, and cakes. There were fortune-telling tents, baubles and trinkets for sale, games of chance and many diverse entertainments. And, of course, there were the animals.

The swarms of people and their activities were an awesome sight. Eventually, having selected a suitable location to meet up with their groom toward the edge of the fair, and incidently near a stall selling more potent libations, they made their way to the livestock pens.

Thea breathed deeply, drawing in the fulsome animal aroma. Bypassing the cows and chickens, they found the pigs. The stoat pens were constructed of low-lying enclosures, formed of rope and wood with the top portion open. Thea very much enjoyed examining the swine as she passed, occasionally stopping to comment with a comely pig's owner.

"Robert!" screeched Jones, to the detriment of Thea's eardrum. The maid waved her arms in greeting.

A shy, tall, gangly fellow came forward and answered her cry.

He bowed politely to Lady Althea, tongue-tied to be presented to the daughter of an earl. But soon enough, he lost his shyness in avid discussion of his pigs. He led them to his pens and she was suitably impressed. These were fine swine indeed. After selecting a couple of likely piglets for future delivery to Steyne, Thea turned to again examine other nearby pigs. There had been one or two that had caught her eye. Perhaps another chance to enhance her papa's stock?

A series of grunts and oinks from a nearby cage drew her gaze to a comely piglet. The pig looked decidedly familiar. Her eyes narrowed as she walked closer to further examine the animal. Then her gaze settled on the blue ribbon collar encircling its neck. There was no longer any doubt when she saw the spot around his left eye. It had to be Egbert, her very own Uncle Egbert. What was he doing here? She looked about the milling crowd of farmers, and found her suspicions justified.

The keeper of her papa's piggery stood nearby, in close conversation with Squire Fossbinder. It was certainly suspicious. Hadn't Papa accused the squire of stealing one of his pigs?

Prompt action was called for, unless she was willing to sacrifice Uncle Egbert. It was one thing to leave him home at Steyne. But leaving him in the hands of a butcher was another. It was likely that he would be sold to some uncaring farmer who would fatten him up and then, most dire of all calamities, devour him.

She had asked her father to take especial care of him and he had sworn he would. Egbert was definitely here without his knowledge. She would soon resolve matters to her own liking.

Checking to see that no one noticed, she took the few steps necessary to reach Uncle Egbert's pen. Then she boldly reached down and grabbed him. Clutching the darling to her chest, she began to run. Jones hadn't noticed her actions, too engrossed in the attentions of her Robert. However, someone did, and that someone warned the pigkeeper.

Shouts of "Pignapper!" and "Thief!" were raised, and Thea increased her pace. She faced an almost solid mass of bodies. She shifted Egbert's weight, which was much heavier than she'd expected.

Slowing her pace slightly, she chanced a look to her rear, but couldn't tell if anyone was in pursuit.

Thea dodged around a large woman wearing a sickly pale green dress, then picked up her pace once more to circle a family group in her path. Intent on searching ahead to catch sight of her groom, she stumbled over a parcel abandoned in the pathway. Thea successfully fought to regain her balance but a stitch in her side made it painful to breathe. She increased her pace before looking ahead, but her forward motion was immediately checked. Her head shot up to discover what blocked her progress. There before her stood an astounded Lord Hartingfield holding her upright.

He glanced at Thea and her burden, and his lips turned into a frown as he looked more closely at Egbert. Surmising that she'd taken the pig without paying for him, he swung the wayward girl into his arms and strode to his phaeton. Effortlessly tossing both pig and girl up into the seat, he tossed a coin to the boy who held his horses and took the reins. Snapping his grays into quick motion, Hart hightailed it out of the area. After putting several miles between themselves and the fair, he halted his high-steppers at the side of the road.

"Thea, I hope I am not abetting a thief. Your explanation, please?"

"It wasn't my fault, Hart. Truly it wasn't." She smoothed back her hair, which had been greatly disordered by her flight. "It's Egbert, you see."

Now he was back to the course on which she usually led him—total confusion. Just who was Egbert and what had he to do with her? "Egbert being?"

Thea lifted up the pig. "I'm sorry. I had forgotten that you hadn't met. Lord Hartingfield, may I present Uncle Egbert? Egbert, this is our savior, Lord Hartingfield." The pig snorted in greeting.

Hart's lips quivered in supressed laughter. He had been jealous of a pig, of all things ludicrous.

"Well, you don't have to laugh at him, my lord," commented Thea, apparently up in the boughs, for fear he might hurt a pig's feelings.

"Ah, Thea sweet, I wasn't laughing at the . . . at Egbert, but at the situation. Now tell me, how long have you two been acquainted?"

"He's been my favorite since his birth. Papa wouldn't let me take him for a pet, although he did promise to take particular care of him while I was gone. I'm certain Egbert's here without my father's knowledge."

Thea clutched Egbert to her bosom, squeezing the piglet too tightly. The pig grunted his displeasure. "What I do know is that Squire Fossbinder was at the fair, in close conversation with Papa's pigkeeper. For sometime, Papa has been accusing the squire of pig-nappery and now it looks as though it is true! I had no choice but to take Uncle Egbert. Otherwise, he might have been sold."

"But what will you do with him?"

"Do you think Aunt Prunella . . ." Thea stopped speaking when she saw the negative shake of Hart's head. "No, I suppose not. A London townhouse isn't the healthiest place for livestock. Perhaps I might hire a carriage to convey him back to Papa?" Again, Hart shook his head. "Well, my lord, what do you suggest?"

It was his own fault. Having saved her, it now fell on his shoulders to play hero to a pig. He addressed the animal, "How would you like to come live in my mews until such time that we may arrange proper transit back to Steyne, Egbert?"

Egbert appeared to acquiesce, as did Thea. "I knew I could depend on you, Hart!" Thea grinned at him. "But you didn't say what brought you here, so luckily close to hand."

"Luck had nothing to do with it," Hart growled. "Mack and I met up with Miss Rawlings at Hatchard's this morning. To my great surprise, she mentioned your scheme to attend the fair today." He rubbed at his forehead as if trying to erase its worry lines.

"You do know how dangerous it was, don't you? I deserted Mack, jumped into my phaeton, and rode hide to leather. And it was a good thing, too. Why didn't you accost your pigkeeper and demand he hand the pig over?"

"I didn't think of that, my lord," she uttered in a low voice.

"Oh no, you don't. It's Hart. And if you ever forget it again or do anything so featherheaded, I'll . . . I'll be tempted to throttle you!"

She trained wide eyes on him. Far too innocent eyes. Falsely innocent. "Why, your face has turned red and the veins are sticking out in your neck, Hart. You must calm down. If I promise to be more careful in future, will you forgive me?" She curled an arm around his, and began to flutter her long lashes at him.

She was handling him again! Blast the chit, he just couldn't stay angry with her. "For a price."

"Price?" Thea's voice squeaked on the word.

He turned and embraced both girl and pig. He then delivered her a most justified set-down in the form of a lingering kiss.

When at last he broke away, Thea couldn't help but sigh. Hart said, "You're forgiven."

The next week seemed like a hurried blur to Thea. Her court presentation had been a tremendous success. At the crowded Drawing Room, the Queen had gone so far as to reach out a hand and acknowledge her by saying, "Lovely. So like your mother. Her presence is dearly missed."

Savoring the success, the household was busy making preparations for the come-out ball for the two young women. While morning mists clung to the air, Thea and Emma were in the midst of their final ballgown fittings at Madame Brandt's popular establishment.

Emma, a model of decorum, remained perfectly still for the dressmaker to place the last pin. Thea, however, squirmed and fidgeted.

Madame Brandt scurried to her side. "*Cherie*, you must remain in place. *Oui*. Let me perform this one little *adjustement*." Her black mop of curls disappeared among the folds of Thea's gown.

Standing motionless, in fear of puncture or worse, Thea asked her friend, "Do we have Sir Oswald on our list, Emma?"

"I believe so. Isn't he the one who has an addiction to high-stakes gaming?"

"Oh, dear. That's right. Well, there's always Lord Phillingim to fall back on. If only his corset didn't creak."

"You still have many other potential suitors, Thea."

Thea turned her head to address Lady Prunella and received a pinprick for her efforts. A muffled voice called out, "*Sacre bleu*! Hold still, *petite*, I am almost complete!"

Again taking the pose of a statue, she asked, "Aunt? Don't you have a nephew?" She recalled her aunt's late husband had an heir in the form of his brother's son.

"Yes . . ."

"Do you think he might do for me?"

"If you favor silly young puppies, certainly. Just now, he has taken up Byron and does his best to stand around appearing melancholy. I have no doubt that with one look at you in the seafoam you are wearing, he'll decide to throw caution to the winds and immediately declare his undying devotion." Her tone deepened. "Most likely, he will write sonnets to your earlobes."

"That bad, eh? At least I'll have one admirer." But perhaps a very young husband might suit her.

Emma asked, "Aren't you forgetting Lord Hartingfield?"

"No, he'll just prop up a wall and glower at me as usual." She bit her lip. "I'll have to see if I cannot stir up some interest from Mr. Covingtree."

"Isn't he the wealthy banker?" asked Emma.

"The one and same."

"Isn't he a bit . . . mature for you, Thea?"

"You think I cannot interest him?"

"Oh, no," reassured Emma. "Not at all. Just would he interest you?"

Thea shrugged, setting off a squeal of exasperation from the harried modiste. Madame Brandt hurriedly tucked one more dart and proclaimed the fitting *finis*.

Chapter Nine

"I cannot believe my good fortune, Hart." Mack spoke only half jokingly. "First I've been accepted for membership at both White's and Brook's, and now I've received a voucher for Almack's." He gazed at the sacred interior of White's and added, "My father will be quite impressed."

"You'll have to spend more of your time in my pocket, Mack." Hart, unaware of the titillating gossip in which he had recently played such an important role, dealt a new round of cards. "You have now gained entré into the veritable hubbub of tonnish society, especially among those with marriageable daughters," he intoned languidly. "They have discovered that you are well set up, the grandson of a viscount, and the close personal friend of yours truly.

You will be feted until you collapse from exhaustion or boredom."

Mack picked up his hand of cards. "Seriously, Hart, I am anxious to attend Almack's tonight. I can hear my mother berating me across the wide expanse of the Atlantic. She would never forgive me if I failed to provide her with a firsthand accounts. She lives and breathes for news of London society." He looked at his cards and laid down two.

"Very well. We will attend, if you insist. But I suspect your wish to appear at Almack's has more to do with a desire to see Miss Rawlings." Hart watched to gauge how his thrust had hit, but it received no reaction other than a studied nonchalance.

Hart dealt him two more cards, and then looked with distaste at his friend's coat. "Are you aware there is a dress code? Do you own any knee breeches?"

"I'll have you know my wardrobe is quite up to snuff, thank you very much. But you cannot truly be serious."

"I am indeed. And we must not arrive later than the very jot of eleven o'clock, for the doors are firmly shut at that time." He scratched his coat sleeve with the cards. "I doubt even the Prince Regent himself could gain access to those hallowed portals if he arrived one minute past the appointed hour."

Mack looked at his hand of cards with undisguised delight. "I can see this will be a most entertaining evening."

"Not if you care for your victuals or gaming. The food is meager and often stale. There is no strong drink and the gaming stakes are a mere pittance. But you are allowed to ogle all the lovelies rigged up in their finery, as they set out to conquer the bidders on the marriage mart."

"Good." He ignored the sarcasm in Hart's voice. "Where shall we dine before attending?"

"I'll have my chef prepare us a sustaining repast."

"I was hopeful you would say that. His culinary skill is sublime."

"As are his wages, my friend. So don't even think of taking him home with you to that heathen country of yours. Now, will you bid?"

As the days progressed, Thea and Emma began the normal whirlwind of the *beau monde*: routs, balls, ridottos, salons, and, of course, shopping.

And then there was that special institution: Almack's. Even the word thrilled Thea. And tonight would be her first appearance. Perched on the edge of her carriage seat, she wondered if she would be ignored by the dandies. Or would she be a hit, proclaimed a diamond of the first water? The possibilities were boundless. Perhaps she would meet him, the man of her dreams. Well, possibly not the man of her dreams, but, at least, the man of her future.

Within minutes, the carriage halted at the revered entrance of their destination. Thea clasped Emma's hand, "I am so excited, I'm sure I will make a fool of myself."

"Don't worry, Thea." Emma gave her a kind smile. "Just be yourself. The young men will not be able to resist you."

Lady Prunella pushed them forward, and at last, they entered the ballroom. Beautiful women clad in magnificent finery and jewels danced with handsome, elegantly clothed men. Others reclined upon chairs, gossiping, watching and being watched. Men and women walked about, greeting friends and acquaintances.

The girls' arrival was swiftly noted. Thea wore a white silk gown with a golden-webbed overdress. Emma was garbed in her favorite rosebud pink. They were delightful additions to the gathering and instant successes. Accordingly, several young bucks claimed their dances. Thea's aunt took a seat with two of the patronesses and looked on with beaming happiness.

Thea granted her first dance to Henry Montgomery, the Viscount Winnwood, Lady Prunella's nephew. And indeed he was a Byron devotee. His face was pale and melancholy, his dark hair tousled and he affected a limp. From the moonstruck look upon his face, it appeared Lady Prunella had been correct: he had taken one look at Thea and felt the tremulous flutterings of new-found love.

In a charming attempt to impress her while leading her onto the dance floor, he softly quoted Byron, "*As midst her handmaids in the hall, she stood superior to them all.*"

Thea wanted to laugh in response. Although the viscount was two years her senior, she felt much older and more worldly than he.

"Thank you for your kind words, Lord Winnwood," she said with a smile.

Forgetting for the moment his morose pose, Lord Winnwood grinned in return. *"And all that's best of dark and bright meet in her aspect and her eyes."*

"Is that from *She Walks in Beauty*?"

"How clever of you to recognize it, Lady Althea."

Their line dance passed pleasantly. Once Lord Winnwood forgot his feigned limp, he danced quite creditably. Thea dismissed her dread over the evening and began to enjoy herself.

At the end of the set, he again clothed himself in melancholy as he escorted her from the dance floor. *"My greatest grief is that I leave nothing that claims a tear."*

"Do not say so, Lord Winnwood, for you must know that I find your acquaintance quite dangerous." Thea gave him a deep curtsey and he bowed politely in return.

"You have conquered my heart, Lady Althea," he claimed with a hand held over his chest.

Then he escorted her back to Lady Prunella's side, where she was introduced to Mrs. Phillipa Cresswell and her daughter, Melinda. A dissatisfied look came over Lord Winnwood's face as he reluctantly escorted Melinda Cresswell into the next set.

Meanwhile, Mrs. Cresswell motioned her nephew, Sir Dudley Smythe, to her side. "Lady Prunella, Lady Althea, and Miss Rawlings. May I present my nephew, Sir Dudley Smythe." Mrs. Cresswell nodded at the handsome young gentleman who towered over them like a wolf amid a flock of sheep.

"Enchanted, Lady Althea." He lifted her hand to his lips and kissed it.

His action appalled Thea. It was not the mode to do other than brush against a lady's hand. His lips were moist and she felt a desire to wipe his touch from her hand. "Thank you, Sir Dudley. You must excuse me, for I see my escort approaching to claim this dance."

She disengaged her hand from his clutch and turned, but Sir Dudley was not to be deterred. "I believe they intend to play a waltz this evening, my lady. Have you already been engaged for it?"

"No. I have not as yet received permission from the patronesses, Sir Dudley."

"Then, may it be my pleasure to sit it out with you?"

Thea was at a loss. She was not sure she liked this man, although with his dark good looks, he was certainly attractive, albeit narcissistic. Why should she avoid him? She nodded in acceptance.

Hart, when he arrived with Mack, was disgruntled to find that Thea was the belle of the night. She was surrounded by not just unlicked cubs and nabobs but several gentlemen of his own set as well. This did nothing to improve his temper. At last, deciding to take measures into his own hands, he commanded, "Come along, Mack." The orchestra had just struck up a waltz.

He weaved his way to Lady Prunella's group and bent to whisper in the ear of Lady Sefton. She smiled and took the arm of each of the young men. They walked directly to the throng surrounding Thea, where she was seated beside Sir Dudley and Miss Rawlings.

"Lady Althea and Miss Rawlings, may I present two gentlemen who wish to dance. You each have my permission." Lady Sefton nodded happily and shooed them onto the dance floor.

Thea hesitated as she watched Emma blush and allow Mr. McCormack to sweep her into the dance. She had no desire to repeat her waltz with Hart. But, seeing they had an interested audience, she realized refusing would create a scene. Besides, she didn't really care to sit out the dance with Sir Dudley.

When Hart swung her into the waltz and placed his palm upon her back, she thought her heart would cease its beat. The room suddenly became terribly hot and she searched for something to say. "You are quite fortunate, my lord."

"How is that?"

"My aunt had the foresight to hire a dancing master."

"Have you so quickly forgotten our previous waltz, Thea?"

She grinned as she deliberately stepped on his foot. Seeing that he intended to ignore her attempt to annoy him, she elected to concentrate upon a spot just below his chin. Then she blushed, becoming aware it was the very spot where she had snuggled when they'd had their first waltz.

"I've decided to revise my strategy, Thea."

"Indeed?" What new torture had the man now devised?

"Yes. I did not intend to accost you at our last meeting, you know. I will forthwith behave with perfect propriety. Now you need not fear me. What think you of my new plan?"

"It sounds very well, my lord. But how can I trust the word of a rake?"

"By making sure that a chaperone accompanies us whenever we are together. I am thinking of putting together a picnic to entertain you. In fact, if you'll bring along Miss Rawlings, I will endeavor to persuade Mack to come as well."

Thea's gaze fluttered to that twosome, who were caught up in the waltz. She frowned. Emma appeared to be enormously enjoying herself. Surely nothing more than friendship had sprung up between her and Mr. McCormack? Ever loyal, Emma would never dream of such a thing, but what of the American? "And who will chaperone them, my lord?"

"Why, we will, of course. If you would feel more comfortable, I can put together a small party. And I am sure Lady Prunella may be prevailed upon to accompany us."

"Thank you, my lord. It sounds lovely."

"Hart. Must I remind you forever?"

Thea peeped up at him. "No, Hart, only when you've fallen from my good graces."

The dance ended. After returning Thea to her chaperone, he spent the balance of the evening propped against the wall and glaring at her many suitors. He was not alone in this endeavor, for Lord Winnwood soon joined him.

On the day of the luncheon al fresco, Thea discovered that Hart had included at least twenty-five people in his invitation. In addition to Mr. McCormack, she was greeted by Lord Phillingim, with his mother, Lady

Phillingim, and Lord Winnwood. Melinda and Mrs. Cresswell were also in attendance, accompanied by that lady's nephew, Sir Dudley.

Earlier, Hart had unhappily discovered the addition of Smythe and Winnwood to his party. Although he considered them little competition for Thea's favors, he would have preferred none. However, he put this thought aside and presented a cheerful face to his guests.

With considerable enthusiasm the party set off for Richmond Hill. Most of the young people rode on horseback; for those who preferred an easier trip, a traveling coach lumbered behind. After an invigorating ride through the green countryside, they found Lord Hartingfield's servants working industriously setting out tables.

"My lord, you have outdone yourself." Thea laughed. "All this for a picnic?"

"Is this not different from our last outing? I was hoping to impress you with my thoroughness and de-sire to please you, Thea. Do not tell me I have failed." Hart mugged a frown at her as he slowly helped her from the saddle.

Feeling rather breathless, she stepped out of his grasp and made use of her fan to cool her over-warm countenance.

"I've yet to meet your friend, Hart," a gentleman called out jovially as he strolled to join them. Hart-ingfield grinned widely at his friend, Lord Harburton, whose arm was possessively held by his intended, Lady Diane.

Once the introductions were performed, they turned to examine the preparations Hart had made. Food had been set out along a long table set with crystal and silver. Additional seating was available to allow more comfort for the older members of the party.

Before long, a rattle of hooves indicated the arrival of the traveling coach and their chaperones. As soon as Lady Prunella exited the coach, Thea darted to her side, followed closely by Hart.

"What think you of Lord Hartingfield's preparations, Aunt?"

"Well done, Hartingfield." Lady Prunella nodded at him with pleasure on her face.

"Thank you, Madam. It is my hope to please you. Might I have your permission to take your niece to see the view?" He turned to Thea. "I have a surprise in store for you."

She cast him a distrustful look as her aunt replied, "That sounds delightful, doesn't it, Thea?"

Thea made a great show of peering at a nearby grouping of trees. "I find the view right here quite lovely."

"Lydia and I plan a prolonged *tete-á-tete*." Lady Prunella's voice was filled with warning. "And you won't wish to miss Lord Hartingfield's surprise." She turned to Lady Phillingim. After seeing that Thea made no move, she turned back and flung out her hands in a shooing motion. "Run along."

Thea had no choice but allow Hart to take her arm. Emma and McCormack were ahead in the distance so they joined Lord Harburton and Lady Diane. The foursome strolled a short distance to see the view.

It was incredible. From the top of a rounded barrow, the countryside spread out below for miles around. The Thames wound softly through a mix of grand houses and thatched huts dotting the embankment.

For a moment Thea imagined she was a bird circling the skies, when a distant building caught her attention. "Why, it can't be." She pointed ahead. "That looks exactly like St. Paul's Cathedral!"

Hart laughed. "That is St. Paul's, Thea. And rumor has it that from this very place, King Henry VIII waited for the rocket announcing the death of Anne Boleyn." He didn't speak for several moments, caught up in the beauty of the panorama. "Do you like my surprise?"

How could she express in words how much she appreciated it? She met his gaze and smiled at him. His eyes reflected pleasure at the sight of her happiness and it was difficult to look away from him, despite the temptation of the view.

It was considerate of him to arrange an outing like this. Emma had thought to bring along their drawing implements, and, although Thea wasn't an accomplished artist, it would be entertaining to attempt sketching the view.

She was beginning to blush at Hart's intent gaze when Mack and Emma strolled over to join them. Lady Diane, Thea, and Emma leaned against an enormous elm tree. Harburton, Mack, and Hart stood talking in low voices.

"Isn't this heavenly?" Emma asked, but she looked at the men rather than the vista.

Lady Diane, too, watched the men. With a sigh she responded, "Yes, simply lovely."

Thea smiled at the two young women who were more interested in the men than in any scenery, no matter how breathtaking. "After our ride I'm famished." Thea raised her voice, "Hart? When will we dine?"

"Whenever you like, my lady." He offered his arm to her and called over his shoulder as they strolled, "Come everyone, we'd better eat before our charming companions become faint for lack of sustenance."

"I'm sure it hasn't yet reached that point." Thea wasn't sure whether to be amused that he wished to please her or annoyed by his joke at her expense. "I am, however, looking forward to discovering the delicacies you have arranged for us."

"Ah, so you aren't faint?" asked Hart teasingly. "If so, I can call for a footman to bring you a biscuit."

"Very amusing. I think I can safely make it the few steps back without need for reinforcement or a battalion of footmen prepared to carry me on the least provocation. However, if I may be so bold, I'm concerned because you, my lord, appear a bit peckish. I shall lend you my arm should you need support."

Hart laughed. "Thank you. How astute you are for noticing my feeble clues. I am reassured that I can count on you for my comfort."

It was in this merry mood that they returned to the picnic site. Thea saw that Melinda and Mrs. Cresswell were already seated at the head of the table where Hart would sit. Judging by Hart's raised brow, some rearranging of place cards had been done by the Cresswells.

When their group passed by Miss Cresswell, who had obviously set her cap at Lord Hartingfield, she looked pleased she'd found a way to separate him from Thea.

The lunch was delicious, although the most formal picnic Thea had ever attended. Throughout the meal, she kept a sharp eye on Hart at the far end of the table.

Miss Cresswell's actions were annoying. The young woman giggled constantly, batted her lashes at Hart continually, and drat if her hand wasn't always creeping over to cover his! Thea narrowed her eyes and glared at him. The cad appeared to be enraptured.

Determined to put him out of her mind, she looked to the gentlemen beside her for distraction. On her left sat Lord Winnwood, who persisted in sending her soulful looks, and on her right was Sir Dudley, who irritated her with inane flattery. In order to shorten the conversation with her tablemates, she ate far more than she should have and her limbs became heavy.

Sir Dudley leaned toward her, with an eye on their host as well. "Lord Hartingfield graciously provided blankets for his guests, Lady Althea. May I obtain one for you to sit upon while you sketch our enjoyable surroundings?"

Thea peeked at Hart. He loomed over Miss Cresswell and appeared to be getting quite an eyeful. What a cur! "An excellent suggestion, Sir Dudley." Perhaps he might be a possible spouse. His looks were such that any young lady might feel herself honored to have caught his fancy. She would add his name to her list of eligibles.

She faced Lady Prunella, just across the table, and asked, "Aunt, may I?"

Aunt Prunella also glanced at the marquess, meeting his eye, before answering, "Very well, Thea. Don't wander too far."

Hart watched their departure with a worried look on his brow, and she turned her head to make a point of giving her undivided attention to Sir Dudley.

Taking up blanket and sketching materials, Sir Dudley shot a satisfied look at Mrs. Cresswell. He led Thea to a glade beside a small pond, perhaps a little farther away than called for by strict propriety.

He spread the blanket, then she took a seat and sorted through her drawing paper. After several minutes of complete silence, she looked up to find Lord Dudley examining his reflection in the pond. She watched as he reached a hand up to smooth his hair and adjust his cravat.

Once he seemed satisfied with his appearance, he joined her by the blanket to watch her sketch.

When a breeze blew up, mussing his hair, Thea half-expected him to go back to the pond to smooth it again. Then, to her relief, she heard Hart's voice.

"I am sure they wandered this way, Miss Rawlings."

"We are just behind the copse, Emma." Thea arose and watched as Hart, McCormack, and Emma rounded the shrubbery.

Hart studied Thea's welcoming expression. "I hope you have been enjoying the day." He saw her smile widen and felt it had been wise to come after her.

"Yes, very much, Lord Hartingfield. Your luncheon has been lovely." Thea placed her hand upon his outstretched arm as he helped her to rise.

Contrary to proper behavior, the Cresswells had brought Smythe along although he hadn't been invited. Hart couldn't help but worry about Thea being alone with such an obvious fortune hunter.

Hart led her a small distance from the others and leaned down to whisper in her ear. "He has not been bothering you, has he?"

"No." Thea peered at him for a moment. "Though I would remind you, I'm quite capable of dealing with him should the occasion arise."

"Good." His face was grim as he continued, "The popinjay wasn't invited. The man's on the lookout for an heiress. Watch out, Thea, he's wasted one fortune already and is on the make for another."

"Thank you, sir, for the unasked for and, may I add, unneeded advice."

"Very well," he replied, smarting slightly from her setdown. At least she was warned.

He escorted her back to the blanket, then turned to address McCormack and Sir Dudley. "I have an urge to explore the bank of the Thames, gentlemen. Would you care to join me?"

As the men departed, Emma pushed aside Thea's sketching pad and sat beside her. "Oh, men! Look at them, off to explore just like children." Emma leaned back and closed her eyes.

Thea laughed, gathered up her pad and pencil and sketched the pond while Emma napped. Time passed quickly. Her drawing was almost complete, and she was reworking a very tricky shadow on the water, only to be startled by the sound of a disagreement.

"Stop that," said an annoyed masculine voice.

"What?" A woman's voice playfully asked, "This?"

Thea turned to Emma as she sat upright. Their gazes locked as they listened in silence.

"Oh, no, you don't!"

"Whatever can you mean, Hart? Surely you want to kiss me as much as I do you," the female cooed.

"Thank you, but I must decline your too generous offer."

Next they heard a scrambling noise. Thea stood upright, ready to march into battle, but Emma held her back. "Perhaps you should stay out of this."

"Very well, Hart." The feminine voice was now cold as ice. "If I have to do this the hard way, I will. No one will believe your word against mine."

Upon hearing this, Emma released her hold on Thea and scrambled to her feet.

Thea was already off in a frenzied rush. On the opposite side of the copse she spotted Hart and dashed to his side. She arrived just in time to see Miss Cresswell tear her own bodice, revealing an expanse of flesh.

"Setting a new trend, Miss Cresswell?" Thea asked nonchalantly as she took his arm.

Miss Cresswell coldly eyed Thea. "Perhaps you might do better to follow my lead, Lady Althea."

Just then, Emma rounded the shrubbery and joined them, taking Hart's other arm.

"Come, my lord, you promised us a stroll," Thea stated, pulling at his sleeve.

Hart couldn't believe it. Thea was rescuing him. It was at that moment when he understood her point regarding Smythe. It was annoying and rather embarrassing to be rescued when he could have extricated himself from the situation.

He observed Miss Cresswell's face turn a very unbecoming red as she spun to address Thea. "Do you think Lord Hartingfield could seriously be interested in a milk and water miss like you?"

"Is that what you believe, Miss Cresswell?" Hart asked imperially as he disengaged himself from her clutches. "I fear you have been misinformed about the subject. Lady Althea outshines you in every way. I'll summon a servant to help you repair your gown." He nodded his dismissal at the woman, then led Emma and Thea through the trees.

"Thank you," he said bringing each lady's hand to his mouth for a gentle brush against his lips, "for your timely intervention." He laughed. "You see, Thea, not every woman feels that a wedding is uncalled for after she has been compromised, even if it's she who has done the compromising!"

Thea quickly glanced around to make certain he hadn't been overheard. How could he bring this up after she had gone to the bother of saving him from that cold-hearted harridan? Thankfully, no one besides Emma had heard his comments. "Is it your turn to try to entrap me, my lord? It will not work, for Emma is privy to all my secrets."

"To all?"

Thea could only blush. Well perhaps, not *all*.

Chapter Ten

The following day, it was late afternoon before Lady Prunella, Emma, and Thea returned home after a productive day of shopping. As Thea walked into the drawing room, she saw a man standing just inside the door.

"Papa!"

Thea flung herself into her father's arms. What a wonderful surprise! "Oh, I am so glad you are here, Papa. When did you arrive? Why didn't you let me know you were coming?"

"Calm down, Thea. Let a father have a look at his daughter." Clutching one of her hands, he stepped back to admire her. "Fine feathers, m'dear." He stepped forward to fold her in his arms.

"I have missed you, Papa. And, you're here. In London. How was your trip?" She wanted all the details about his leaving Steyne. Had it been horribly difficult after so many years? Had he been frightened?

"The roads were much better than I'd been led to believe. And the cattle available at the post house much finer than I expected." He grinned at her. "It's good to be back in town. You were right, m'dear, once I had settled upon the journey my fears evaporated. You see before you a new man."

"Papa, I'm so glad. Welcome to London." A gentle nudge from her aunt forced her awareness that they blocked the doorway. "Aunt, Emma, look who's here!"

Aunt Prunella handed her gloves to a footman as she entered the drawing room. "We heard, dear. Welcome to London, Bremington. What brings you to town so precipitously? No problems, I hope." She signaled that they take a seat.

"You look quite hale, Lord Steyne," commented Emma with a smile which encompassed both Thea and her father.

"Yes, perhaps it's this clean London air?" joked the earl. Then he turned to his daughter. "Thea, dear, I'm sorry but I have bad news. It seems I have misplaced Egbert."

Thea's face lost all expression as Lady Prunella asked, "Uncle Egbert? Didn't he pass away a few years back?"

"No. It's her pet pig. Though why she named him after Egbert is beyond me."

"Her pet pig!" Aunt Prunella's eyebrows disappeared in her hairline.

"Do not be upset, Papa." Thea finally spoke up. "I recovered him, you see."

"You recovered him, Althea?" he asked suspiciously. "How did you know he had gone missing?" Her papa's voice was quiet but she knew he spoke in earnest.

"It is a long, involved story." Could she evade his question? The answer would likely provoke him. "Surely you are too weary from your journey to want to hear it now?"

"No."

"But first, I must ask how Mimsie and Meg are faring, Papa." Perhaps she could distract him from the subject of Uncle Egbert.

"Meg is recovering nicely, Thea. Now, do go on, m'dear." Papa was up on every suit.

Thea capitulated with a sigh. "Very well." It took a moment to organize her thoughts in putting the tale in the most favorable light. "Lord Hartingfield and I recovered him at a country fair where he was being offered for sale by your pigkeeper and Squire Fossbinder."

Lord Steyne bounced off the sofa, outrage evident in his expression. "What? That bast—er . . . dastard. He stole one of my pigs!"

"Bremington, you require some rest after your journey." Lady Prunella spoke soothingly, for he looked likely to expire of apoplexy at any moment. "I am sure Thea will be more than happy to relate the balance of her tale later this evening."

Steyne took a moment to calm himself before replying, "Very well, Prunella. I do need some rest.

But," he directed a stern look at Thea, "I will hear the rest of this story later."

Over the next days, Lord Steyne proved to have gained a new zest for life. He had come out of his nine-year, self-protective shell with fervor. Thea watched his transformation with wonder touched with happiness, although she felt a deep sense of loss. It now appeared he no longer needed her to look after him. She chastised herself for being so selfish. His new outlook forced her to take a deeper look at what she wanted for herself.

She wanted love. A love like her mother and father had shared, a love extending beyond this life into the hereafter. She wished to love deeply and be cherished in return. She wanted a husband and family to look after and in turn, to look after her.

And so, with mixed feelings, she watched her father make a new life for himself. In the mornings, he would devour a hearty repast and seek out old friends, visit his clubs, or participate in whatever diversions town had to offer. Additionally, he diligently began refurbishing his own Grosvenor Square mansion. Much shopping and consultation was necessary in order to render it habitable.

At Aunt Prunella's insistence, Steyne remained in residence in her home until the renovations could be completed.

In the late afternoons, he frequently returned to escort them, at the most fashionable hour, on a drive through the park. This day was no exception.

Thea, Emma, and Lady Prunella were in fine fettle that afternoon as they returned from their ride with flushed faces and cheery dispositions.

The late post had arrived, bringing Emma a letter from Charles Fossbinder.

Thea said, "Come along, Emma. We need to change and then you can read it."

Reaching their suite of rooms, they found Jones waiting for them. She'd already laid out their gowns for the evening and stepped forward to help them remove their garments.

Emma was the first to be suitably dressed and she took a seat in the sitting room while Thea finished dressing. Idly, she opened the letter from her betrothed.

When Thea entered the room a few moments later, she found Emma slumped forward on the settee, in a near swoon. "Jones, fetch smelling salts at once," she called out as she ran to her friend's side.

"Emma!" She patted the young woman's hand with her own. "Whatever is wrong?"

Emma's face was completely devoid of color. She handed the letter to Thea.

Thea searched Emma's face before she looked down to scan the letter. Her surprised gaze shot back to her friend's face. "A baroness, Em? You will be a baroness!" For, through a cousin on his mother's side, Charles had come into an unexpected barony. He was now Lord Gibbons.

Why was Emma distraught? Jones returned with the vial of salts. Thea took the vial and waved it beneath

Emma's nostrils. The color slowly returned to the young woman's face.

"Thank heavens, Emma. You are feeling better now?" Thea dismissed Jones and helped her friend to sit upright. She could not understand her. "Don't you wish to be a baroness?"

"It isn't that I don't wish to be a baroness, although it does enter into it, Thea," Emma whispered. "I am so confused." A tear slid down her creamy face like a dewdrop captured by a rose petal. She stared into Thea's eyes. "You did not finish Charles' letter. He asks that I reconsider our betrothal."

Shocked, Thea read the rest of the letter.

"You know he would much prefer to marry you. But he simply wasn't eligible. Now he is. Don't you see, Thea? I should release him."

Thea scowled as she finished reading it. She studied it once more, as if expecting its contents to have changed from what she had read seconds before.

Her friend had been created for happiness, for peace, for serenity. How could the scoundrel hurt her this way? She had thought him the kindest of gentlemen, but his actions were neither kind nor gentlemanly. Had she been completely wrong about the man?

"But, Thea! My parents! I know they will disown me if I do release him. Particularly now, with a title within their grasp." Emma buried her head within her hands and began to sob.

"I have quite given up on the idea of marrying Charles. So don't be absurd, Emma." In fact, no thoughts of Charles had entered her head for quite some time and she no longer carried about that heavy feeling in her chest.

"In fact, I am unsure now if I ever truly wanted to." Automatically, she handed Emma her handkerchief. "The inexcusable gall of the man! I always considered him quite godlike in character, yet I now find him sorely lacking." Thea tapped the letter against her jaw. "So you see, Emma, you must not break off the engagement on my account, for I do not love him."

"You may be able to fool other people, Thea, but do not try to fool me. I know you love him."

Thea shook her head.

"You truly do not?"

"Truly."

"I've been wondering if I—" A discreet tap sounded at the door, interrupting Emma.

It was that staid and stately butler, Phelps. "Excuse me, Lady Althea. Lord Steyne requests your immediate presence in the drawing room."

Thea whispered to Emma, "Do you want me to stay?"

"No, Thea. You go on. I feel the need for some time alone, to think matters over."

Thea asked, "Are you sure?"

"Yes." Emma nudged Thea's arm. "Go on, Thea. Don't keep your father waiting."

Thea rose and smoothed her skirts in one supple gesture. "Very well. I'll check on you later."

Her thoughts were in a whirl as she descended the staircase behind Phelps. She was no longer in love with Charles. Had she ever been?

Had she merely been in love with an image of perfect manhood, gleaned from her favorite novels? Charles possessed few of those attributes she and Emma had ascribed to him. No, she was not in love with Charles, had never been in love with him. Papa was right. Dreams of marriage to him had been simply that, childish daydreams.

Entering the drawing room, she saw that her papa was not alone. He stood in casual discussion with that venerable gentleman, Lord Phillingim, who stood upon seeing her. Unconsciously, she crinkled her nose at the overwhelming perfume reeking from his person.

Giving an abbreviated curtsey, she said, "Papa. Lord Phillingim, how do you do?"

He, too, sketched a bow then addressed her father. "Sir, if I might proceed?"

Her father shot Phillingim a dubious look before smiling warmly at her. "Excuse me, dear." He walked to the door. "Lord Philligim wishes speech with you." He nodded to a footman, who discreetly closed the door behind them.

Whatever could he want? They had little in common. She sat on a Sheraton arm chair. "Pray be seated, my lord."

Instead, Lord Philligim's corsets protested as he flung himself at her feet. With enormous fat fingers, he grasped her hand and pulled it to his lips.

Red-rimmed pale blue eyes looked up to watch her expression. "Dare I hope that you are aware of my sentiments, Lady Althea?"

Thea pulled at her hand, saying, "Pray, my lord, get up."

"You are an innocent, my dear. I have sent you many gifts indicative of my regard, specifically the book of poems. Might I hope that you perceive how strongly I feel about you?"

Of course she remembered the stodgy book of poems, as well as the candy and flowers. All had been suitable for a much older lady. And all had been appropriately acknowledged at the time.

As he continued talking in this vein, Thea allowed her thoughts to wander back to Charles and how she had ever believed herself in love with him.

For the first time, she had to face the future without that anchor. And what would replace it? Could she consider a life without marriage, without children, without love?

Hart had proved this an impossibility. His kisses made her yearn for more. Even in her naiveté, she was blushingly aware that enjoyment of kisses didn't mean she was in love. Her life would be much easier if only she was in love with one of her suitors. Could she, as many of her peers had done, undertake a marriage without love?

Her thoughts drifted back to Lord Phillingim. The man was spouting poetry from that cursed book of poems. She gave him an encouraging smile and went back to her cogitations.

Hart, the rakeshame, had claimed her lips but she would not allow him to claim her hand. He'd only park her at one of his country estates, expecting to turn her into some brood mare, while he continued with his philanderings. He would rob her purse, her love, her soul, and give nothing in return. Except those kisses.

No, she would not think of that. Anything but recall the tenderness of his lips as they caressed hers. She would have to consult her list of eligibles. Surely one of the gentlemen could claim her love?

"Lady Althea," Philligim called out rather brusquely. Thea realized he must have asked her something but she hadn't a clue what it could have been.

"Come, Lord Phillingim, arise." Feeling somewhat guilty for having ignored him, she flushed.

Pausing a moment to send her a peculiar look, he released her hand and obeyed, bowing deeply to her before seating himself on a small red velvet sofa. His clothing squealed and Thea was hard put to stifle a giggle. Lord Phillingim was a most correct, stuffy individual. However, he rivaled the Prince Regent for girth, without the royal name to protect him from ridicule. She suspected he, like the Regent, would like to imprison people who poked fun at his size. But she had to admit a certain fondness toward him, for in some lights the gentleman resembled her dear Uncle Egbert.

"Lady Althea, I ask again," he pulled at his vest, "will you please consent to be my wife?"

So this was what he had asked! She searched her mind for something to say.

"My Lord, this is so sudden."

"No, Lady Althea. The emotions you evoked within me were sudden, but I assure you that I have come to you with much thought, cogitation, and even prayer. I feel certain we would suit each other. We are both of fine family and estates. While my income does not equal yours, I am fully capable of administering to the needs of a greater estate." He took a moment to clear his throat.

His purple-hued vest was so constricted that a button had come undone. A bit of white shirt winked out at her. Here was her first real proposal, a moment young ladies all dream of, but instead of the penultimate romantic moment of fantasy it was pure farce. At least she had to give him credit for being honest about her fortune.

"If I may be so bold," he continued, "I would like to state that your loveliness and liveliness are a great attraction to me. And, if you do not love me now, perhaps with time you will find that you may. Please, say you will be mine."

He struggled to raise himself from the sofa, rolling from side to side. Thea signaled him to remain seated. His mother must have rehearsed him, for he'd never previously spoken to her at such length. "Very prettily said, my lord. I recognize the great honor you are offering me, however, I feel we would not suit."

"Please do not be too precipitous, Lady Althea. Mayhap upon reflection you will reconsider. Shall I give you more time to weigh your decision? I hope to convince you that my admiration is true and that you can return my sentiments."

"As you wish, my lord. Yet I would warn you I do not anticipate a change in my decision." Thea bowed her head to hide her expression of amusement.

Not wishing to hurt his feelings, she waited until the sound of his footsteps faded before she laughed aloud. The man knew nothing about her other than her pedigree and her finances. Why, even Lord Hartingfield knew her better. She immediately sobered as she pushed this thought from her mind. Were all men of the *ton* so obvious, callous, and indifferent?

And, what of her resolve to fall in love and marry? Couldn't she have worked up a reasonable regard for Lord Phillingim? She shook her head sadly. There was no way.

Chapter Eleven

Thea fidgeted on the carriage seat. Hart had escorted Aunt Prunella and herself to an enlivening performance of the opera. Emma had begged off again and Thea worried about her continuing melancholy over the letter from Charles.

Hart sat across the carriage in light conversation with her aunt. Thea idly glanced out the carriage window. A deep baritone rang out, claiming her attention.

"Drrrink to me onnly with thine eyes." Two men, gentlemen by their dress, gamboled aimlessly along the sidewalk, serenading the street.

"There's no other like Rosieee!"

As their carriage passed the men, one of them stepped off the curb and stumbled. He would have fallen but for the timely intervention of the other man. Her eyes widened as she recognized him.

"Why, it's Papa! Stop the carriage!"

Hart calmly tapped on the roof of the coach and it lumbered to a halt. He stuck his head through the window and eyed the gentlemen. One of the men doffed a hat from his head and saluted their carriage while the other continued to sing about the charms of Rosie.

"I do believe. Oh." Hartingfield blinked then looked again. "Yes, it is he. The gentleman wearing the watchman's hat is," his voice broke, "my father, the duke."

"Squigy?" Aunt Prunella squeezed past him to gaze out the window. "Do not be facetious, young man, the duke is assuredly quite ill." She looked out. "Oh my."

"My father appears to be on the mend." He watched with disbelief while the duke executed a leap with a clicking of his heels. It was too much. With a groan, Hart clapped a hand over his eyes.

Thea grinned. This was too good to be missed. "Yoo-hoo, Papa," she called with a large wave, gaining her father's immediate attention.

"Why look, Squigy. It's my lovely daughter." He strolled over to the carriage, swinging his watch fob and humming beneath his breath. The duke joined him.

"So this is the enchantress," the duke glared at Hart, "I have heard so much about. Pleased to meet you, Lady Althea." He took her hand and gave it a resounding smack of the lips before turning to the earl.

"You know, Beamer, if I didn't think you'd have my head, I'd try to cut out this unlicked cub." He nodded at his son. The nod sent him momentarily off balance, and he clutched Steyne's arm for balance. He then smiled at Thea. "What say you, my lady? Would an older gentleman have a chance at winning your hand?"

What a delightful man. She grinned back. "Certainly, my lord Duke, if my papa approves."

He poked an elbow into Steyne's ribs. "At least your gel's got spirit, Beamer."

Hart, who'd been silently moaning into his neck cloth during this exchange, uncovered his eyes and raised his head as Lady Prunella spoke up.

"Squigy? I still cannot believe my eyes," she simpered. "I was under the impression you were gravely ill." She batted her eyelashes.

The duke leaned against the carriage. "No, Prunella, it was all a rus—" The word ended in a cough. His gaze landed upon Hart and he seemed to recollect himself. "No, dear lady, I am quite recovered as you can see." He performed a quick jig with his feet.

Hart swung open the carriage door. "Join us, won't you?"

"Glad to oblige you." Both men entered the carriage as the duke continued speaking, "By the way, can you settle a dispute we are having? Beamer insists that the next stanza is about Rosie's fulsome beauty but I say it is the one about her roving eye. What say you, son?"

Hart shrugged at Thea, then answered, "I believe the next line pertains to Rosie's one true love."

"Quite right, Hart! I knew her roving eye wasn't next." Lord Steyne settled down into his seat next to Thea. "I'm glad you could join us on this auspicious occasion."

Thea bit her lip to keep from laughing. This was the first time she'd seen her father in such altitudes but she rather enjoyed it. "Why auspicious, Papa?"

"Tonight, kind relatives and friends, I received the coveted *Sacred Order of the Pig.*" He bowed his head in reverent silence.

Everyone murmured sounds of approval.

"Congratulations, sir," said Hart. "And Father, how delightful to meet you in such good health."

"Yes, m'boy. I know you were surprised to see me here in town," spoke up the duke.

"Oh, no, Father. I wasn't wondering at all, especially since at our last meeting I was informed you were on your last legs."

"I have made a remarkable recovery, have I not?" The duke paused to clear his throat, then, less than discreetly, changed the subject. "I came to attend the annual meeting of our society. I must remain circumspect and not divulge the name of our group but I do feel it appropriate to give you a little hint." His voice reduced to a loud whisper. "It is an offshoot of the Gentlemen's Philharmonic Club!"

Thea didn't know how to receive this information. She had, of course, heard of the Philharmonic Club. But what, pray, had it to do with pigs? She glanced at Hart for some clue, but his smile was lopsided, reflecting his confusion.

Her father reached across the carriage to tap the duke on his knee, missed, and landed in that dignified gentleman's lap. "Excuse me, Squigy." He swooped to retrieve the duke's hat, which had fallen from his head.

As Thea helped her papa sit up, he said, "Squigy, tell them of the honor you received."

"Ah, yes." The duke brushed his hands down his lapels. "I, too, received a great honor this night." He repositioned the watchman's hat on his head, giving it a jaunty angle, then peered in the eye of each person within the carriage, as if to guarantee their attention, before continuing. "You are looking at the new *Grand Hyena*."

Aunt Prunella's reaction was all the man could have hoped for. Her voice was breathless with adulation as she cooed, "Squigy! What a wonderful distinction!"

"Thank you. Thank you." He bestowed a regal smile on his most appreciative audience. "Indeed, you may be proud."

"I am." her voice was low. "I have heard that the Grand Hyena has numerous social duties."

"Yes, Prunella, that is correct."

"You will have to host several dinner parties?"

Thea watched their byplay with amusement. Whatever was her aunt hinting at?

"Indeed I will," replied the duke.

"In that event," Aunt Prunella peeped coquettishly in his direction, over her unfurled fan, "will you not be requiring the services of a hostess?"

A week later, as Phelps showed him into Lady Prunella's town home, Hart noted a slight lessening of the formality that was the butler's usual mien. Perhaps it had something to do with his daily calls? Or that often Thea seemed pleased with him and allowed him to stay for tea?

His courtship of her was endless. He had laid his heart, his happiness, his future in Thea's palms but still he could make no headway with her. She remained adamant in her refusals to consider his offer. Possibly today something would change. Certainly, matters could not be much worse.

On this occasion, she received him with a smile and an extended hand. Did he note a fond gleam in her eyes?

"You are looking lovely today, Thea." She looked like springtime personified in a jonquil day-gown with wisps of white flowers adorning her bosom. He fought an impulse to take her into his arms. Most likely he would have, if Lady Prunella had not been seated just behind them.

When Thea glanced in the direction of his hand, he looked down at the carefully chosen book of Shakespearean sonnets he'd brought. He offered it to her and enjoyed watching her face light up when she saw the title.

"Thank you, Hart. I will find great pleasure in reading this. You know how fond I am of his work."

At least, he knew how fond she was of quoting Shakespeare. He only hoped it hadn't been a mistake to give her more armament.

Their visit passed far too quickly. He repressed a sigh. It was nearly impossible to press his suit when she was constantly surrounded by relatives or callers.

Preoccupied with his thoughts, Hart did not notice a gentleman ascending the stairs immediately in front of him. A near collision ensued.

Shaken out of his reverie, Hart recognized Thea's farmer. Whatever was he doing here? "How do you do, Mr. Fossbinder?"

"Quite well, quite well, Lord Hartingfield. I have the pleasure of informing you that I am no longer Mr. Fossbinder. I am now Lord Gibbons."

"Ah, so you are the cousin who inherited the barony? My felicitations, Lord Gibbons." Hart could not keep a cynical note from creeping into his voice.

Lord Gibbons apparently missed the underlying sarcasm. In a pompous tone, he announced, "I am calling today to request the fair hand of Lady Althea. So perhaps I may be so forward as to suggest that double felicitations are in order?"

Hart's stomach clenched. He repressed the desire to harm the buffoon on Thea's doorstep. Perhaps he should call him out. Turning to do so, he discovered that Gibbons had disappeared into Lady Prunella's townhouse.

Blast it all. Thea would agree to marry that social climbing, prosing upstart. And it had to happen just when she'd begun to accept him. Well, that put paid to his courtship. However unlikely, matters *had* become much worse.

Determined not to be such a cawker as to sit and watch her with her new lordling, an image which skewered him like a knife, he considered leaving London. Neither Thea nor the other members of the ton would have the pleasure of watching him defeated in his one attempt at love. Yes, he would leave. Had not a sojourn in the country been his intention before he had met this hoyden? He would depart at once for his father's country estate.

Within the town house, a short time later, Thea was notified that Charles Fossbinder, Lord Gibbons, had come to call. "Where is he, Phelps?"

"In the hall, my lady." He displayed no emotion but she wasn't fooled. It was obvious he didn't approve of Charles.

"How appropriate. Thank you." She turned to her aunt and asked, "What think you of this development?"

"I find the whole situation distasteful, Thea. His behavior toward Emma has been most ungentlemanly and I would prefer not to meet the man. You are quite capable of handling him, are you not?"

"Yes, Aunt." Thea watched her aunt's departure, and left to her own devices, fanned the embers of resentment and anger. Why did he have to come to town? Was it not enough that he'd made Emma so wretched? Must he pour salt into the wound? Emma loved him and he was a most fortunate man to have gained such loyal affection.

Thea gave him a social smile as he entered the room. "How do you do, Lord Gibbons?"

He laughed. "Such formality, Thea? And no chaperone? Is this what fine London society teaches our young ladies?" He stepped forward to capture her hands. He then swung her arms wide and did a careful survey of her, eyes moving slowly from top to toe. "You look quite the lady, my friend."

Heat traveled into her face and she abruptly snatched her hands away. "I understand congratulations are in order, Lord Gibbons. Have you come to discuss wedding arrangements with Emma?"

"Miss Rawlings has most graciously terminated our betrothal. I have come to discuss wedding arrangements with you."

Surprised that Emma had not informed her of the ended betrothal, Thea quirked an eyebrow in imitation of Hart at his most top-lofty. She turned to a sidetable, picking up the book Hart had brought her. "And who is your chosen bride, my lord?"

Charles brought his hands to her shoulders and spun her around, giving her a shake. "Enough shilly-shallying, Thea. If you expect me to perform the pretty, going down upon one knee, then you are well mistaken. You know you want me, and now that I have acquired the title, there is no impediment standing in our way. Your father agrees."

"You have spoken with my father?" She couldn't believe the preposterous conceit of the man. *You know you want me*, indeed! Wishing to physically distance herself from him, she moved toward the hearth, Hart's book clutched to her bosom. The fire blazed brightly, quite like the fury inside her. "You spoke with my father before making sure of my feelings?"

"I knew your sentiments and I met him on my way in just now. It makes all the difference having his approval. My acceptance in society will soon follow."

That tore it. "Why, you son of a pignapper! Charles, you are the most conceited, self-consequent fellow— and I say fellow because I cannot bring myself to refer to you as a gentleman—I have ever had the misfortune of meeting. I would not have you if you were the last man on this planet. Now, please leave." Thea took aim with her book and started to throw it. She hesitated before launching the missile, for she didn't wish to damage the book.

Charles looked relieved as she carefully laid it down. Then before the smile could leave his face, she snatched a bronze figurine from the mantel and launched it instead. Without breaking, it barely missed her target and bounced off the heavy paneled door behind his back.

"Do not be so precipitous, Thea. You know you love me. Do not do anything now that will embarrass you later." He extended his hands to her. "Come, if you really desire it, I will make my offer to you with all the stodgy formality at my command. My father nearly plagued me to an early grave, so much did he desire the match between Emma and me. My heart was broken along with yours."

Was it possible he loved her and was willing to act less than honorably in pursuit of a happy solution to their estrangement? She thought not. Rather, it was most likely he loved her purse and her social position more than honor.

"Leave, at once." This was the second proposal she had received in this room—how many more was she destined to suffer?

He didn't go.

"I said, *leave*. If you do not go, I will call Phelps and have you bodily removed." She lifted another figurine as if testing it for weight.

"Calm down, Thea." He darted behind a chair. "If you truly do not want me, I'll have to accept it. But I will not spend months courting you." When Thea failed to respond, his voice became peevish as he asked, "Might I see Emma?"

Surely he wouldn't? "You think to change her mind about your betrothal?"

"Since you will not have me, I am certain her family will be quite relieved to find that our engagement can be resumed."

Did he think such a threat would force her to change her mind? "We will see about that. Emma will no more have you than I will." She only hoped she was correct. Poor Emma had been so troubled by thoughts of her parents' probable reaction. However, even Emma could not look upon Charles with anything but disgust since his true character had come to light.

Thea yanked the bell-pull.

Phelps immediately answered the summons. Had he been standing just outside the door and listening? Most likely, otherwise he would not have been so prompt. The perfect butler was human. Thea winked at him. "Please ask Emma to join us, Phelps."

"I am sorry, my lady, but Miss Rawlings is not at home." As he spoke, there were sounds of laughter in the hallway. All heads turned to see Emma enter the room with Mr. McCormack.

"Did I hear my name?" Emma called out gaily, then she caught sight of Lord Gibbons and her expression became guarded. Her gaze flickered to Mr. McCormack, as if seeking reassurance.

He smiled down at her, then placed his arm around her shoulders. "Have we come at an inopportune moment?"

Phelps stepped into the breach. "No, sir. Lady Althea was just asking for Miss Rawlings." He left the room after carefully replacing the bronze figurine from whence it had come. Thea noted that he made certain the door remained minutely ajar.

She turned to find Emma conversing with both men. Thea saw the assessing looks each one gave the other. At any other time she would have found the situation amusing. But not now.

"Emma, I would speak with you," Lord Gibbons said, command in his voice. "Alone." His eyes glinted when he looked at McCormack, as if willing him to disappear. Thea stood ready to come to Emma's defense but found it was not necessary.

"Thea and Mack are my dear friends, Charles. Whatever you have to say to me," she smiled sweetly at him, "they are most welcome to hear for I shall certainly discuss it with them."

Gibbons' lips gaped open, giving him the look of a shocked fish. "As you wish." He hesitated and his jaw clenched before he continued, "Might I have the pleasure of your hand in marriage?"

"Aha," Emma answered. "So Thea declined your offer?"

He shot her a look of fury before nodding.

"And what makes you think that I would have you?" Emma appeared to be deliberately baiting the man.

"It is my fondest wish and hope that you will for-give me and that your affection for me remains un-changed." His eyes hardened as he added, "And your father . . ."

"Ah, yes. My father is hopeful to see the last of me, is he not? Well, he should be quite satisfied when he receives my letter informing him of my betrothal—to Mr. McCormack." Emma gave Mack a dazzling smile. "So you see, I'm afraid I must decline your gracious offer, my lord."

Gibbons' face turned red with unguarded anger. He raised a fist, and for a moment Thea wondered if he meant to harm Emma. Then, dropping his arm, he turned on his heel and marched from the room without further ado. Once the doors were firmly closed, Emma laughed nervously and Thea soon joined in.

"If you had only seen your face, Thea! I cannot believe you did not suspect my regard for Mack."

"And I cannot believe the way you stood up to the knave! '*What makes you think that I would have you?*'" she mimicked her friend. "I felt uncertain whether I would scream or laugh aloud."

Mack grasped Emma's hand and then led her around the room in an impromptu dance while Thea watched their antics.

Still, this development did not resolve her problems. They still loomed heavily over her future. It was for-tunate she had finally discovered Charles' true nature but her quandary remained. Could she find love before it was too late?

Chapter Twelve

As much as possible, Hart wiped the moisture from his brow. Most assuredly, that blackest of moments in the lifetime of mankind, the veritable pit of existence, had descended upon him, an event he'd never contemplated.

For hours he'd trudged along in silence, sloshing through deep rivulets of water. The storm had almost passed and every pore of his body was waterlogged. His jacket, a once lovely creation by one of London's superior tailors, now drooped disconsolately over his head like a nun's veil. His carrick greatcoat, with its several capes, became increasingly heavier with each pace he took.

And to complete his misery, he had lost not only his love, his future, but he had then been set upon by cutthroats, who had stolen his beaver hat and purse as well as his most favored horse. Unfortunately, they had not taken his life. He'd wanted them to but they sought only his valuables.

He saw a flicker of light ahead and breathed a heart-felt sigh. The inn. Warmth. Safety.

Without a ha'pence to his name, it was likely they'd turn him away. Would they believe his tale? There was no other choice but to take his chance on it. But with his run of foul luck, he'd probably find himself sleeping in a hayloft.

He increased his pace until one boot, once a fault-lessly shiny Hessian, became mired in mud.

Lord Harburton's ball had been a tremendous success for everyone but Thea. She, Emma, and Lady Prunella were exhausted as they entered their carriage for the ride home.

Thea was particularly annoyed. Last night, Hart failed to attend Lady Henry's ball after requesting that she save a waltz for him. And today, he had not made his usual afternoon call.

Tonight his absence was most notable of all, for the host was his particular friend and she suspected her family's invitation had only been extended at Hart's instigation. She had received several pitying looks. Most irritating of all had been Miss Melinda Cresswell's reaction. Not only had the schemer cut her, she had turned to Lord Philligim and announced in a deliberately loud voice, "Hart tired of her soon enough!"

When the threesome arrived home, wearied and glad the night was over, Aunt Prunella said kindly,

"Thea, I'd like to speak with you, if you do not mind." She turned to Emma and added, "Goodnight, dear."

Thea followed her aunt to her sitting room. At her gesture to do so, Thea took a seat, carefully avoiding the crocodile chair. Why was it necessary that they talk in private?

"Thea, I am concerned. Tell me, please, have you and Lord Hartingfield had a squabble?"

"No, er, yes." How could she explain to her aunt that they *always* argued? However, the last time she had seen him, she thought they had gotten along fairly well. "I do not believe so, Aunt."

"Then how do you explain his absence?" Lady Prunella looked at her inquiringly.

"I don't know that I can." Thea's voice wavered. "Perhaps he finally came to realize I will not marry him." She avoided her aunt's gaze.

"Ah. I begin to understand. You are upset because you sent him about his business and now you find you miss him."

"No." Thea traced the edging on a delicate candy dish. "I'm afraid that's not it at all, Aunt."

"Then tell me, child." She reached a hand out to grasp Thea's. "I hope you know I am quite willing, anxious in fact, to stand in place of your mama. I can see you are suffering and perhaps talking about it can make it better."

How could she tell her aunt what the real problem was? What would the reaction of any decent lady be upon learning her niece was a wanton who exchanged kisses with a man she didn't love? Aunt Prunella would send her back to Steyne in total disgrace. "I'm afraid talking about it will only make matters worse."

"You do know you may trust me, don't you?"

"Of course I trust you." She gave her aunt's hand a squeeze. "I simply do not wish to lose your affection."

"I cannot think of anything which you may do or say that could cause me to feel less affection for you."

How she wished she could believe that. Thea fell forward from her seat and into Aunt Prunella's waiting arms. Her scent evoked long forgotten memories of Mama, who also had worn the faintest touch of hyacinth fragrance. Tears sprang forth from Thea's eyes and she was unable or unwilling to staunch their flow. "I, I am a f–f–fast woman."

"Now, Thea, everything will be all right." Rather than evicting her from the house as she'd expected, Aunt Prunella patted and consoled her until at last, she felt much calmer. Her tears had been soothing.

Pushing herself upright, she used her handkerchief to dry her eyes. "You must think I am the veriest peagoose, Aunt. I never cry."

"No, dear, I do not. What I do think is that the time has come for plain speaking. You must tell me exactly what has led you to believe that you are fast. I may be able to help." Aunt Prunella gave her a coy look. "You see, I was once a young woman like yourself."

Thea responded to the love in her aunt's voice. She found herself telling of her experiences with Hart and how, whenever they were alone, it seemed inevitable that they kiss. And how ashamed she felt.

"That chicken-wit! I cannot believe such an experienced man of the town could botch something so simple as this. Thea, the man is absolutely lovesick over you." She saw the negative shake of Thea's head. "Yes, my dear, he is. And, since he is as inexperienced in love as you are, he is behaving like a complete nodcock."

"I'm sorry, but he is only offering for me out of a misguided sense of honor."

"Nonsense. That may be what he tells himself to rationalize his actions, but the true state of his heart is plain to see."

"But, Aunt, his reputation as a man-about-town would indicate otherwise."

"Exactly so, my love." Aunt Prunella sighed. "Can you not perceive the difference?"

"You mean attraction rather than love?"

"I am not certain those are the words I would have chosen, but yes, that is what I mean." She looked her in the eye. "But, tell me, do you not feel any similar affection for him?"

"I hadn't thought so. You see, for years I simply knew I was in love with Charles Fossbinder." Thea rubbed her index finger against the grain of the velvet upholstered chair. "Through his recent actions toward Emma, I now know I was in love with a dream. I looked for kindness, I found kindness. I looked for patience and generosity and that is what I found. But it was all an illusion, an illusion of my own making. How can I ever again be certain of my own heart?"

"I believe you will know." Lady Prunella's smile was radiant as she added, "When I received a kiss from the right man, I knew it."

Fascinated, Thea asked, "Had you ever experienced any kisses from the wrong man, Aunt?"

"Too many, my dear. But that does not concern us now. Allow me a day or two to think. We'll see what I can come up with. You may depend on me to think of something."

How relieved Thea felt. She hadn't realized how much she missed having a mother with whom she could share her thoughts and from whom she could receive advice. "Very well."

It had helped to discuss her problem. Yet, she did not feel quite comfortable with the idea of relying on her aunt. It was not in her nature to totally rely on anyone. After all, could she not find a way to interpret her own heart?

Upon Hart's arrival at the inn, the innkeeper greeted the blue-faced nobleman with jovial familiarity. Hart soon found himself ensconced in that gentleman's finest guest room and promptly fell asleep amid crisp white sheets.

Stark sunlight, dappling his face, awoke him the next morning. Tenderly stretching exhausted muscles, he carefully sat up. He saw that his mud-stained garments of the night before had been carefully laundered and left folded over the fireplace fender to dry. A man's dressing robe lay upon a chair.

He bravely donned the robe that evidently belonged to his host, for it was many inches too small. A round-faced serving maid knocked as she entered the room with a pitcher of warm water. His host was most conscientious. The maid left with promises of returning with a large breakfast.

Hart performed his ablutions and had just completed the task when the maid returned. He sat and poured himself a cup of tea. The delicious aroma permeated his senses and extended a sense of warmth and well-being.

He had been a fool. He should never have left London, should never have left Thea in the hands of that coxcomb. Hart didn't care to admit it, but he loved her. A restoring night's sleep made it clear to him she loved him as well. She was simply too stubborn to admit it.

It was not too late to return and rectify matters. She might have accepted an offer from that jumped-up turnip but there were still banns to be posted, wedding plans to be made. It was not too late. If necessary, he would kidnap her.

Perhaps he wasn't as clearheaded as he'd thought.

A day later, Hart wasn't in much better spirits. He found himself seated in his dining room with Mack amid the clutter of earlier bacchanals.

"For heaven's sake, Hart. Haven't you moped enough?" asked Mack. The other guests had long since departed and he watched Hart through worried eyes. He'd never before seen his friend in such a grim mood, a mood Hart hadn't thrown off since returning to town. If only the man would talk about whatever was bothering him.

"I suppose you're right." Hart twirled the empty snifter between his fingers, his gaze concentrating on the tiny drop of fluid remaining in the bottom.

"This was supposed to be a party celebrating Emma's acceptance of my offer, you know." Mack glared at him. "Snap out of it, man! Aren't things prospering between you and Lady Althea?"

Hart's lips tightened and he swallowed before answering. "I ran into Fossbinder a few days back and he as much as told me that they are betrothed."

"Nonsense, Hart. I myself was present when she sent him to the rightabout. Emma, too. The fellow acted like the complete cad and I was relieved to see that those two young women finally recognized him for what he is: an unfeeling scoundrel."

Hart sat as still as the night. He no longer listened to his friend. Instead his heart sang joyous tidings and the chorus blocked all other sound.

Yes, he'd made an utter nodcock of himself. But, at least all was not lost. He could still convince Thea of their mutual love. Suddenly, anything was possible.

Early the next morning, Hart sent a note to Thea, requesting she accompany him for a carriage drive that afternoon. He had missed seeing the minx. Perhaps she felt the same way and would reconsider his proposal.

Upon receipt of the note, Thea turned to her aunt for advice.

"I think you should go, my dear. For the more time spent in his company, the more clear your heart should become."

"Very well. I shall send my acceptance." But, she thought, the dastard had some explanations to make.

When he arrived that afternoon, Hart was dressed as impeccably as usual. For all his experience, courtship of a woman was an area in which he lacked competence. There was too much at stake. Why had he ever allowed her to creep into his heart?

Thea was attired in her favorite green pelisse, set off perfectly by a chip-straw bonnet with feathers dyed to match. The set of her lips, however, did not auger well for the afternoon's enjoyment.

"Have you come to gloat, my lord?"

"Gloat?" He had no idea what she was talking about.

"Well, since all the latest *on dits* about town concern your tiring of me so quickly, I felt sure that was your purpose."

"I am pleased to hear that you missed me, Thea. I do apologize for my prolonged absence." Hart hesitated before adding, "I missed you, too."

She didn't answer.

Hart's heart pounded. He wasn't quite sure how to approach the subject of the lack of privacy they would have on their ride. She'd most likely think her proposed curricle companion had been brought along as a calculated insult.

No young society miss would approve of him. However, Thea was quite unlike any other girl, though entitled as any to her position within the *ton*. If only they could talk, he felt certain matters could be suitably resolved. If he could explain the current situation. "I have unexpectedly hired," he cleared his throat, "well, I hired a new groom."

"How lovely for you." She looked at him as if his wits had gone begging and, for a moment, Hart wondered if she was correct.

"I mean, he's in my curricle and, well, you might not care for his appearance."

"Oh, is that all? You should know that would not put me off, Hart. I would like to get this drive over with. Shall we go? And you may introduce me to your new retainer." Thea nodded pertly as she took his arm and led him to the outer door.

Hartingfield swallowed. She could always refuse.

Phelps opened the door and bowed discreetly as they approached. The staid butler straightened abruptly and his eyes widened in astonishment as they lit upon the scene in the street. Lord Hartingfield's first-class racing curricle and gorgeous matching chestnuts were being held by a scrawny, bedraggled street waif.

Thea, too, saw the boy and turned to Hart with a delighted grin. "My lord, your new retainer?"

Hart smiled in relief. He should have known she would not fail him, but there was one more test to come.

"Henry," he called as he led Thea to the horses' heads. "Lady Althea, I would like you to meet Henry," he tried to continue but the child rudely interrupted.

" 'Enry, Gov'ner, 'Enry. I've tried an' tried to tell you me name is 'Enry. You know, after the King!"

"My apologies, 'Enry. Thea, I am pleased to present 'Enry to you." Grinning wickedly, he studied Thea's expression. It was one of utter amusement.

Hart helped her climb up. Then he turned to Henry. The boy glanced uncertainly from him to the curricle seat, next to the tiger perch behind, and then back to Hart.

"Still unsure about the height, 'Enry? Well, take up your previous position and I'll let you try driving my rig."

Henry gave a beautiful gap-toothed grin. "Thank 'e, Gov! It's 'onored I be, Gov!" He slithered up into the curricle.

When the odd threesome were settled, Henry sat between Hart and Thea. Hart conscientiously checked for traffic then handed the reins to the boy, being careful to show him the correct method for holding his fingers.

The boy was a natural and although Hart sat tense beside him, ready to take over if the need arose, Thea settled down to enjoy the ride. After a few blissful moments, he handed the reins back to Hart and then wriggled back onto the curricle seat.

Crinkling his nose, Henry commented to Thea, "You smells just like a lady ought ter, mum."

"Thank you, 'Enry."

"There's only one smell I likes on ladies better." Henry nodded his head.

"What is that?" asked Thea.

"Fish. I just loves the smell o' fish."

Having received a proper setdown, she laughed delightedly. Hart, too, threw his head back in amusement.

The boy looked up at them reproachfully before he continued, "That's 'ow me mum smelled afor she passed to 'er just reward."

Thea sobered instantly. "Have you any family, 'Enry?"

"No, mum. I kin take care o' meself."

"Well, 'Enry," replied Hart, "I hope that you will not regret your agreement to work for me, for I am sure you will make a fine groom."

Again, Henry gave his gap-toothed smile. The lad could not have been older than six or seven years and Thea's heart went out to him.

"How did you come to employ such a valuable groom, my lord?" Thea asked over the top of Henry's head, which only reached her shoulder. The boy avidly watched the sights of London as they tooled through its busy streets.

"The rapscallion jumped into the middle of the road, directly in the path of my horses. Then, just as I thought we'd drive straight into him, 'Enry vented an unusual whistle. My horses stopped dead in their tracks and allowed him to pet their noses. It was a most bewildering moment but I knew that 'Enry had found his calling. I will personally supervise his training."

"A most wise decision, Hart." Thea was proud of him. He had shown great generosity and kindness of spirit in taking up the obviously unloved and poorly fed youngster.

Several moments later he murmured, "Thank you, Thea."

"Why, whatever for?"

"For understanding." Hartingfield was smiling but completely serious.

Thea answered him with a "Pish." She turned to admire the courageous, although filthy, boy who had survived on the mean streets of London. "Do you like animals, 'Enry?"

"Yes, mum. I sleeps in a stable not too far from 'ere and sometimes they lets me feed their cattle. That's 'ow I learnt me whistle."

"Tell me, 'Enry." Thea grinned widely. "How do you feel about pigs?"

Chapter Thirteen

A mood of comfortable silence filled the sitting room. The only sounds emanated from the gentle fire crackling in the hearth and the soft breathing of the two young women, seated side by side. Thea sat placing stitches in a sampler while Emma popped sweets in her mouth as she idly looked over the latest fashions in *La Belle Assemblee*.

Disrupting the quiet, Emma turned over another fashion plate, covertly watching her friend through hooded eyes, then blurted out the subject that had been on her mind, "Admit it, Thea. You have grown quite fond of Lord Hartingfield."

Disconcerted, Thea stabbed herself with the needle. She mumbled while sucking her finger, "I am not certain 'fond' is the correct word. My attitude is more one of armed truce than fondness."

"I disagree with you there. Didn't you tell me how fine and generous a man Lord Hartingfield is revealing himself to be?"

"Yes." Thea went back to her sewing. If she was honest with her friend, she would admit to a growing *tendre*. But it was a far cry from that greater emotion, true love. "It would appear that you and Aunt Prunella have similar opinions."

Discarding the sampler, she faced her companion. "She suggested that I am not fast, merely in love with him. Do you think she is correct?"

"It seems possible." When Thea said nothing, Emma demanded impatiently, "Well, are you?"

"After the fiasco with Charles, how can I ever be certain about my sentiments toward any man? I can no longer trust my instinct, since my imagination is apt to provide whatever a gentleman may be lacking."

"I think you are being too hard on yourself."

"Perhaps. Aunt Prunella assured me that I would know my feelings when I kissed the right man. But she also said she had kissed many wrong men. I, however, haven't kissed anyone but Hart. So how can I compare?" Thea's voice became a whisper. "I only know that when he kisses me, I turn into an unresisting idiot who melts at the warmth of his touch."

"Maybe you should try kissing someone else then."

Thea gave Emma a penetrating look.

"Don't even think of it! I was making a jest!" Emma jumped from the settee.

"If only there were someone with whom I could safely test my feelings."

"Is there no one on our list for whom you might feel some affection?"

Thea thought for a moment then shook her head. The most suitable gentlemen were either far more interested in their hunters than her or else appeared to be self-satisfied wretches. There was little choice between the two lots.

"In that case, you might as well kiss the first man who asks you to dance at the ball tonight," replied Emma. She gasped at her words, evidently regretting them.

However, Thea didn't react rashly, as she would have in the past. She'd learned to think before reacting. "I shall simply have to learn some other way."

A thousand twinkling candles illuminated the cavernous ballroom within Lady Prunella's home. A majestic orchestra played softly in accompaniment to the sounds of arriving guests. Large bouquets of flowers stood in urns and vases, sending a pleasant floral scent wafting through the household. The family stood at the entrance of the ballroom, a few marble steps above the main room, welcoming their guests. Just behind them, an impressively garbed footman bellowed out the titles and names of the latest arrivals.

Lord Steyne had put his foot down. The girls' come-out ball would not include any gypsy accoutrements. Instead, it would be a quiet, elegant affair. As indeed it turned out to be. Subdued guests, sparkling in their finery, milled about the room.

Mrs. Cresswell, unbecomingly dressed in a pale green and purple gown, had taken up a position not far from the receiving line, surveying each new arrival and passing out praise or pity, whichever she deemed appropriate. Melinda, as always perfectly attired, and the new Lord Gibbons, looking his handsome best, stood nearby, tolerating Mrs. Cresswell's peevish pronouncements.

"Here comes Lady Pemberton with her youngest chit. She managed, with virtually no dowries to speak of, to fire off her four eldest girls quite creditably. While this child's a beauty, she's also a proper frip. I think she can look much higher this time around." Mrs. Cresswell's gaze turned back to her daughter and family friend. "Ah, that reminds me, Melinda. Tonight you will begin cultivating the acquaintance of Lady Althea Candler."

The young woman gasped. With a level whisper, she demanded, "Whatever for, Mama? She holds it within her hands to utterly ruin me."

"That is exactly my thinking, daughter. However, if you are on terms with her, she will be less inclined to destroy your reputation. I know we may depend on Lord Hartingfield to say nothing." Her lips twisted. "His code of honor will prevent it."

"I cannot see why that would stop him," said Gibbons. "He would most likely enjoy the sport in destroying," his tone became malicious, "a paragon like Miss Cresswell."

"If you do not understand," replied Mrs. Cresswell heatedly, "then I'll not trouble explaining it." She waved a garish orange fan to cool her heated cheeks. "Do not despair, Melinda. You will come about. And

Lady Althea is our first step. Look, she's coming this way."

The older woman unhappily noted that Lady Althea, attired in a pale green lace concoction, looked especially radiant. Like diamonds, mischief glittered in her green eyes and an attractive smile lit her face.

Mrs. Cresswell had been disappointed in her nephew, Sir Dudley. He hadn't put himself out at all in pursuit of Lady Althea. When he refused to come to the ball tonight, she'd wanted to throw up her hands in exasperation.

But then, another thought had occurred to her. Charles Fossbinder, Lord Gibbons, had recently come into the title. Using her connections with his mother, she'd been able to accept her invitation with him serving as escort. Now, if he'd only do what he'd agreed to do: remove Melinda's competition, namely, Lady Althea.

He'd implied, and she was rather inclined to believe him, that the girl thought herself in love with him. It shouldn't be too difficult for him to place her in a situation that would necessitate their marriage. Then the field would be clear for Melinda to go after Lord Hartingfield. Yes, it was a clever plan.

"Careful, young ones, on your toes." When Gibbons failed to move, Mrs. Cresswell prodded him in the back. "Do not forget the fortune that will be yours if you can but achieve her hand, young man. It is far too large to whistle down the wind. We will begin, Melinda, by your passing her this note."

*   *   *

Thea and Emma joined Mr. McCormack beside a potted palm. Emma, who had received disgruntled approval from her family, planned to have Lord Steyne announce their betrothal later this night. She was in high spirits, dimples showing.

Emma was the first to see the approaching Cresswell party. "Don't look now, Thea, but those awful Cresswells are coming this way with Charles in tow. Perhaps, if we move away, we can avoid them."

"*We* have done nothing of which to be ashamed." Thea bestowed a cool smile on the Cresswells and Lord Gibbons.

"This is a delightful gathering," said Charles as he bowed to the group, but had eyes only for her.

"Aunt Prunella has outdone herself," replied Thea. "You look lovely tonight, Melinda."

"Thank you," Melinda replied as her mother and Lord Gibbons moved on. "Your gown is lovely."

"Why, thank you." Thea wondered why Melinda had chosen to remain behind until the young woman thrust an envelope into her hands.

"I rely upon your good nature," was Melinda's cryptic reply as she turned to rejoin her mother.

Thea glanced at the note, then moved to a remote corner where she could examine its contents. After quickly scanning it, she was more confused than ever. Why did Melinda wish to meet her in the library? Perhaps she was embarrassed by her behavior in attempting to attract Hart and wished to tender an apology? Although, any apology should be directed to Hart rather than Thea. Perhaps Melinda feared Thea would spread gossip about her and wished to ask that she remain quiet.

Thea's brow creased as she glanced about the crowded room. Whatever the reason, she had little choice but to agree to the *tete-á-tete*.

As the clock chimed the hour, Thea glanced about once more to make sure no one would notice her stealthy departure. Papa had announced the engagement between Emma and Mack, who were now dancing and fortunately attracting everyone's attention.

She would meet Melinda, discover what she wanted of her, then return to the ballroom as soon as possible. Her aunt appeared to be in rapt discussion with her cronies and for once there would be no interference from Hart because he'd not made an appearance. Blast the man.

Accordingly, she slipped into the corridor.

Upon entering the library, she was taken aback by how shadowy and dark the room was. She called, "Melinda?"

Instead of the young woman, Thea was startled when Charles stepped from a shady corner of the room. In one hand he held a snifter of her aunt's fine brandy, and in the other, a lighted cheroot wafted a thin trail of smoke. He doused the cheroot in the brandy, the sizzle loud despite the noise from the nearby ballroom.

"Have you seen Melinda?" she asked, uncertain why she suddenly felt unsure of herself and the situation, as if something was amiss. Completely losing her courage, she spun to leave the room.

"Ah, Lady Althea," said Charles silkily. "You don't mean to leave so soon? I'm sure Melinda will arrive shortly."

Thea turned back, undecided whether she should stay or go. Courtesy demanded that she at least speak to him. "I am sorry," she said, eyes gazing at the Aubusson carpet beneath her feet, "but I find this rather awkward. Please excuse me."

"I have thought many things about you, Lady Althea," he cunningly replied. "But I never thought you fainthearted."

"I am not fainthearted."

"Then why are you leaving?" he demanded. He closed the distance between them and took her arm. "Come, cry friends. Although my heart may never recover, I hope you will retain a small corner of your heart for the boy who shared your childhood episodes."

She felt herself weakening.

"Melinda assured me she would soon join us." When Thea hesitated, he positioned himself between her and the door. "Pray, tell me about your stay in London. I'm sure with all its entertainments, you've found many things of interest."

Thea sensed she was being manipulated but did not know how to avoid it. "It has been exciting but my schedule has been so crowded with social events, I haven't had much time to see the sights. Have you visited any of the museums?"

"No. I'm afraid that never piqued my interest." He closed the library door. "But I am ever open to new ideas." He came forward and placed his hand beneath her chin. Lifting it, he looked directly into her eyes. "Are you?"

"Yes. No. I don't know." She stepped back into the room, but Charles didn't release his hold on her. Instead, he pulled her into his arms, encircling her waist.

Hart's embraces had never been like this. He had never forced her to do what she did not wish.

She tried to push away, pummeling Charles with her fists, furious that he would force an embrace in this manner, furious with herself for being in such a predicament, furious that she had not realized, until now, this very moment, that she was in love with Hart. Drat the man, where was he when she needed him?

Charles continued his crushing embrace, bending her back over his arm at an awkward angle. She lost her balance and rather than continue fighting him, she found it necessary to clutch his lapels if she did not wish to end up on the floor. He bent closer to steal a kiss but she turned her face away. Then she heard the door open.

Thank goodness, rescue at last!

Lord Hartingfield arrived at the ball with a harried look on his face. Lord Steyne immediately came forward to greet the late arrival.

"Hart, I'd given you up!" His father, the Duke of Devonshrop, stood by Steyne's side, looking as if he'd like to throttle his son.

Steyne welcomed him with a hearty back slap, almost knocking Hart's breath away.

Grimacing, he answered, "I regret my tardiness but I was delayed by a matter of business." Surely it wasn't stretching the truth too far. After all, when Henry had run off after dark in search of a missing Uncle Egbert, it had been imperative that the boy be found forthwith. Of course Egbert was soon located in Hart's study. But it had taken the greater part of an hour to locate Henry.

Hart's eyes scanned the crowded ballroom. "I am certain Lady Althea has been proclaimed an unqualified success." He turned back to the men. "Where may I find her to bestow my congratulations?"

"I might have known it wasn't my company you sought." Lord Steyne laughed.

"Yes, she is a success," announced the duke. "She's here somewhere." He waved an arm about the ballroom. "As you said, Lady Althea is an incomparable, a veritable diamond. I was afraid you'd choose some namby-pamby schoolroom miss for a wife." His tone grew warm. "I am pleased to know you have followed in my footsteps and exercised the utmost in good taste."

"She hasn't yet agreed to have me, you know."

His father looked at him with disappointment. "Of course she will have you. You're the heir to a dukedom, for heaven's sake! Though, that didn't count for much with her mama, did it, Steyne?"

The earl shook his head. "She'll make up her own heart, title or no."

"Do you need some hints," asked the duke, "for the proper way to conduct a courtship? I assure you, Steyne and I would be most pleased to advise you in any way."

"Thank you, Father, but no. I will persist." He directed a solemn smile at the earl. "A great authority on matters of love—Mack, to be exact—has assured me that persistence pays off."

"Perhaps you should have consulted him earlier. I wish you luck of it," said his father with a hearty grin.

"You're most likely wishing us to Hades," Steyne added with a knowing look. "Keeping you here jabbering this way. Be off with you and do your best, it cannot fail."

"Thank you for the encouragement, gentlemen." Hart swept his gaze over the guests, when Lady Prunella caught his attention. He quickly joined her. "You have outdone yourself, Ma'am. And, may I say you are in looks, as ever, this evening."

"You, as well," Lady Prunella replied absently then returned to her perusal the room. A worried furrow etched her brow. "Thea disappeared from the ballroom some moments ago, Lord Hartingfield. I believe she entered the library. And I also believe that Lord Gibbons was already in that room. Do you comprehend my concern?"

Hart's jaw tightened. "Has anyone noticed her absence?"

"Not yet, but I fear they soon may."

"Do not worry, Lady Prunella. I will see if she requires my assistance."

"Thank you," she replied with a smile. "That quite eases my mind."

The orchestra struck up a waltz. People appeared from nowhere and the once merely crowded ballroom became insufferably congested. Hart crossed the room, and with every step, some individual would call to him, laying claim to his attention. When he thought he had run the gamut, having achieved the entrance to the hallway, he nearly collided with Mack and Miss Rawlings.

"Hart," said Mack in a friendly voice. "I was sure we would eventually have your company this evening." Emma stood by his side with a fretful smile. She glanced to the library door and back at Hart.

Was she concerned about Thea? Or was she worried he'd find her? "I understand Lady Althea is in the library. If you will excuse me, I must be on my way."

Emma insinuated herself between the hallway and him, shaking her head. "I shouldn't go in there, Lord Hartingfield."

"Whyever not?"

"Thea is not alone."

Hart pushed past her, "All the more reason for my timely intervention." Mack and Emma followed him, quite like a mother duck with her ducklings, he noted with a grim smile and pushed open the library door.

An unappetizing tableau met his gaze.

There before his eyes, stood Thea entwined in the arms of that doltish farmer, both caught up in an enraptured kiss. He felt the presence of the two behind him, the solidity of the floor beneath his feet, the current of warm air as it circulated the room, but his head had been stuffed full of cotton wadding. He couldn't think what to do next.

One minute, he felt he should intercede, then the next he wanted to throttle her. Perhaps he could debonairly ask if they wanted some privacy?

Emma, whose face turned grey, observed the tableau with Mack from their positions just within the doorway. They were soon joined by a worried-looking Lady Prunella and an ecstatic Mrs. Cresswell.

Hart took one last look at the enraptured couple before stalking from the room. Thea had been telling him the truth: she was not in love with him. In fact, he now wondered if she kissed all gentlemen with such enthusiasm.

He'd accused her of being stubborn but he was the one who was pigheadedly arrogant. Why he ever imagined she could love him was beyond reasoning.

The women who had been chasing him from youth onward had amply demonstrated it to him, if only he had paid attention to the lesson. He was lovable only for his title and his wealth. At least Thea had been honest in her dealings with him. She'd always said that title and wealth were not what she wanted. She wanted love and now she appeared to have found it—in the arms of some other man.

Thea squirmed, trying to find some way to escape Lord Gibbon's clutches. Out of the corner of her eye, she saw Hart arrive and her muscles relaxed imperceptibly. He would put paid to her attacker.

But, no. He was leaving. How could he leave and not help? Thea tried to call to him, but Charles took advantage. He quickly covered her mouth with his own, effectively silencing her calls for help.

By now thoroughly fed up with his unwanted embraces, she reacted to this invasion with unbridled fury. She bit down on his lip—hard.

Charles yelled and released her, toppling her to the floor in an ungainly heap. When it became obvious that he would do nothing to help, Mr. McCormack and Emma stepped forward to help her in rising.

"You bit me," cried Charles. He raised a handkerchief to his mouth.

"I most certainly did. You deserved it." Her fury remained unabated. "You wouldn't release me." She looked at the others: Emma, Mack, Aunt Prunella, and Mrs. Cresswell. "Now, if you will excuse me, I must find Hart."

Mrs. Cresswell stepped forward and grabbed her forearm. "Not so fast, young lady." Leering, she added, "It appears that a betrothal is in order."

"Whatever do you mean?" Thea whirled to remove the woman's hand but the woman just clamped down that much harder.

"You were caught *en flagrante* with Lord Gibbons. I think the consequences are quite obvious."

"Obvious, my eye. The man was attacking me."

"It didn't look like that to me from the way you clutched his lapels. Look, they are still creased from your handling." Mrs. Cresswell pointed at him.

Thea spun to take in his appearance, and he did appear to be the worse for her handling. She felt particularly proud of his swollen lip.

Charles shook his head, then dabbed at his mouth with his handkerchief. He'd changed his mind about wedding Thea. No fortune was large enough to convince him to spend his remaining years under the cat's paw with her. She'd probably beat him senseless within a sennight of their wedding. She'd always been able to best him.

However, he didn't wish to be accused of behaving in an ungentlemanly manner. As he removed the handkerchief from his mouth, he wisely held back a reply until he could resolve the issue in his own favor. He signaled Mrs. Cresswell to dispense with their plan to force Thea into marriage. But the woman was too caught up in the drama of the moment.

Mrs. Cresswell's voice became louder. "You have been compromised and you will marry Lord Gibbons or forfeit your position within society, Missy, that I know for sure!"

And Thea, in answer to the woman's words, unthinkingly flung back her own, "I'll have you know I've already been compromised—by Lord Hartingfield! If I could not be coerced into marrying him then I certainly will not marry Charles."

Hart, who had tried to leave but hadn't been able to rid the image of Thea from his head, had returned to the library in time to hear Thea's proclamation. Something about the way Lord Gibbons had held Thea bothered him and he'd eventually seen through the jealousy fogging his brain. Thea hadn't been a happy participant. Now, his peripheral vision took in the number of other people who had come to witness the scene. Their numbers now included Lady Sefton, Lady Jersey, Lady Phillingim, and Lord Steyne.

He opened his mouth to explain because if someone didn't do something, Thea's reputation with the *ton* would be destroyed. However, Thea caught his eye. She smiled warmly at him and he realized, in that instant, that what she felt for him ran as deeply as his feelings for her. In that moment all eyes in the room turned to watch them grinning like children at each other.

Thea was the first to recover at least somewhat. "My dear Lord Hartingfield, will you do me the pleasure of becoming my husband?"

The inhabitants of the room inhaled a deep breath of shocked silence, until at last Lady Sefton laughed kindly. "She's utterly captivating, Lord Hartingfield. No wonder she stole your heart."

"That she did. Although why she couldn't have accepted one of my numerous proposals and chose this particular moment with an audience, is beyond me. If you will excuse us? I wish a few moments alone with my betrothed."

He waved his arms for everyone but Thea to leave the room and for once, she appeared eager to be alone with him.

In the corridor outside the closed library door, Aunt Prunella turned to deliver a setdown to Lord Gibbons. "How could you? You actions were not that of a gentleman."

"My lady," he said with his most endearing bow, "you are correct. I was overcome by the loveliness of Lady Althea and in a moment of passion declared my love." He spread his hands in an entreating gesture. "I am most ashamed and regretful I overstepped the bounds of propriety and I ask your forgiveness. It will never happen again."

He paused to judge the effect of this pronouncement upon the persons present and felt that it would serve. To give his pose further credence, he added humbly, "I shall now go forward and do good works to atone for my impudence. Please say you forgive me, Lord Steyne and Lady Prunella." He bowed his head.

"Very well, we shall speak no more of this matter," answered Steyne haughtily.

"You ninny," Mrs. Cresswell growled. "You almost had her purse within your hands."

"Better to forfeit her purse than forfeit my life, madame," he answered in an undertone. Just when the notables present had begun to think he might not have behaved so abominably, the woman had to ruin it all by reminding them of what he had to gain. The scandal would be the delight of the *ton* for weeks to come.

Without considering what it would do to his injured lip, he signaled a footman to bring him a fresh brandy just as the milling crowd began to disburse.

Chapter Fourteen

Alone at last in the library, Thea's eyes rounded in surprise as Hart lowered his lips to hers. He pulled her into his arms and kissed her as thoroughly as only a reformed rake could when embracing the woman who'd captured his heart. She encircled his neck with her arms and returned his kiss with joyful abandon.

When Hart moved to tenderly kiss her forehead, her eyes lit in amusement.

"You have been compromised, my lord. You never answered earlier. Have you reconsidered your decision?" She enjoyed turning his own words back on him. "Will you agree to an immediate betrothal?"

His eyes crinkled in amusement. Two could play this game. "My answer remains the same."

Thea placed her palm against his cheek. "Shall I force you to reconsider, Hart?"

Again, his lips claimed hers. He bundled her more tightly into his arms, as if he never intended to release her.

After many contented minutes, Thea sighed as she snuggled delightedly into that precious spot beneath his chin. "I love you, Hart," she whispered.

A huge boyish smile lit his face, "You are not marrying me for my title or wealth?"

Thea shook her head.

"You are not marrying me to avoid the censure of the *ton*?"

"No."

"We are making a love-match?"

Thea's voice was as soft as a cashmere shawl. "I hope so, Hart. I sincerely hope so."

He looked deeply into her eyes and she knew the truth of her love for him was written on her face.

"Of course, I haven't told you of the depth of my esteem, have I?" said Hart teasingly.

Thea looked at him in shock. Had she been mistaken? Or was the cad playing with her? Blast the man and blast her heart for loving him so. "No, you haven't."

Hart lifted her into his arms, pulling her feet off the floor. He swung her dizzily about the room, his voice a low growl. "I love you, Thea. I'll never stop loving you."

Sometime later, the two lovers were interrupted by the sound of the door opening. They looked up to see Lady Prunella, the Earl of Steyne, and the Duke of Devonshrop watching them with warm affection on their faces.